C☕FFEE BREAKS

Short Stories

COFFEE BREAKS

Short Stories

CAROL WHITE

Library of Congress Cataloging-in-Publication Data

White, Carol
Coffee Breaks: Short Stories

p. cm.
Paperback ISBN: 978-0-9975470-6-I
Ebook ISBN: 978-0-9975470-7-8
Library of Congress Control Number: 2017941099

10 9 8 7 6 5 4 3 2 I
First Edition, June 2017

 CITRINE PUBLISHING

Boca Raton, Florida, U.S.A.
561.299.1150
Publisher@CitrinePublishing.com
www.CitrinePublishing.com

Also by Carol White

Hidden Choices

From One Place to Another

Sitting Pretty

A Divided Duty

To Lisa and Pamela

MENU

COFFEE BREAKS

Short Stories

GONE CAT

My parents live in an oceanfront mobile home community called Sandy Shores, which is in southeast Florida about thirty miles north of Fort Lauderdale. At my father's retirement party a year ago, he announced to a room full of friends and relatives that he and Mom had sold their house in upstate New York, bought a double-wide, and were heading south to spend their golden years in the Sunshine State. I was about to ask Mom and Dad if they were crazy when I saw them gazing into each other's eyes. The only crazy thing was the love they still shared after thirty years. I wasn't as lucky. My two-year marriage to Kyle Morgan had ended after an unsuccessful reconciliation, and I'd hardly dated since my divorce.

"We want you to come visit, Brooke," Mom said. "Sandy Shores is a perfect location. You can walk to the beach, and the town has the most amazing little boutiques."

My mother was now in the middle of her sales pitch, and there was no stopping her. After she finished, I chimed in.

"Sounds great," I said, immediately dismissing the idea.

After my college graduation, I had moved to a small, yet serviceable, studio apartment in Brooklyn Heights. Kyle moved in with me after our wedding, but when we split up I kept the place and continued commuting into Manhattan, by subway, to my job as a restaurant reviewer for *Around-Town Magazine*. Many of my meals were taken care of, a perk of the job that had landed an unwelcome ten pounds onto my small frame.

"And wait till you see the beautiful church we have," Mom went on, already making the decision for my first visit. "It serves our community, but everyone's welcome. Even tourists stop by because it's so famous, and we have a wonderful chaplain. We just call her Barbara because it's very casual here."

Mom thought she was adding sprinkles to her ice cream sundae of an invitation, and I didn't have the heart to disillusion her. I rarely attended church because I wasn't ready to give up sleeping late on Sundays.

My parents adjusted quickly to Florida, and had made many new friends within the tightly knit community. One Sunday, Mom called to tell me that their next-door neighbor, a travel agent, managed to arrange a three-week trip to England for fifteen Sandy Shores residents, including my parents.

"It's a great deal, Brooke," said my mother, with a laborious sigh. "Dad and I are dying to go, but there's a problem."

I didn't have to listen to the rest of the conversation to know what the problem was. It was Marac—their cat.

"You know I won't leave him alone, and if he gets out I can't ask my neighbors to run after him," Mom whispered, as if this were a world-class secret. "I'll bet you haven't had a vacation this year, and I hear it's awfully cold up in New York."

Before I had a chance to devise an excuse to get out of cat-sitting, my father took over the phone.

"Hi honey, tired of New York yet?"

Dad asked me that every time we spoke, and my answer was always the same.

"Not yet, Dad, but you'll be the first to know," I said, and we both laughed.

"Brooke, your mother is looking forward to this vacation. It's the first time we've ever been to Europe, but she won't leave Marac. Please say you'll come down and stay. Our place is easy to take care of, the car is here for you, plus there's a handyman who lives down the block if anything goes wrong. And don't be shy. Everyone is very neighborly in this community," my dad said.

"Tell her about the church social," my mother said, loud enough for me to hear without the phone. "Wait, I'll tell her myself."

"Brooke, your dad and I won't go on this trip unless we know Marac will be taken care of. He's such a sweetie and we simply can't put him in a kennel," my mom said defiantly.

Now it was my turn to sigh, but I knew I had to help out.

"Okay, Mom. Email me the dates and I'll make a reservation," I said.

"Thank you, sweetheart. Daddy will pay for the tickets. Oh, I almost forgot. There's a luncheon every Sunday right after services," Mom said. "The entire congregation is invited."

My mother never forgets anything.

"Mom, I'm not sure about the church thing, so please don't push it," I said.

Silence.

"I've already told Barbara that you'd be thrilled to bring along a cake from one of your own recipes. Oh, dear, I'm sorry. I guess I should have waited to hear from you," my mother said.

"Mom, I'll make the trip, but I'm not falling for the guilt one," I said.

"Okay, you'll decide when you get here," Mom said.

After another twenty minutes of conversation, in which she mentioned the church social about a dozen times, we hung up.

I had reluctantly agreed although I knew the time off would do me good. My mother could drive me crazy at times, but there was no question that Mom and Dad had been wonderful parents. It really wasn't a big deal to go to Florida and I knew they were anxious for me to see their new surroundings.

February in New York had been a bitter month and March didn't look like it was going to fare any better. Palm trees and beaches started to sound appealing. There'd be no blind dates, no singles functions that my boss was always suggesting I attend, just sun and relaxation for three weeks. I'd be able to catch up on my sleep, except for Sundays when I'd been assigned to baking duty for the church gathering. I'd worked so many hours of overtime that my boss was cool with giving me an extra week off in addition to my regular paid vacation time.

Because I had to eat out five or six times a week, it was almost impossible to start a healthy food plan (the word "diet" was not in our industry's vocabulary) in New York, but during my stay in Sandy Shores I'd be able to walk to the local grocery store for fresh fish, salads, and vegetables. I'd swim in the ocean, and finally begin work on writing my own cookbook. I guess going to church once in a while wouldn't hurt either, plus it would be a good way for me to try my hand at some new desserts.

There would only be one drawback to my vacation—the reason I was taking it in the first place. Marac. Marac was short for Marathon Cat. He was the fastest runner I'd ever seen, and any open door or window was an engraved invitation for his exit. Dad had told me that Jesse, the community handyman, had installed a special double door in their new home to keep Marac inside, but I'd seen that cat get out of tighter situations.

My parents met me at the Palm Beach Airport and I had to admit they looked terrific, Florida style. They were both dressed in printed tropical outfits, including matching straw hats, which covered Dad's balding pate and Mom's newly acquired blond bob. They seemed happier than ever. We caught up during the car ride back to Sandy Shores.

"Wait till you see your room," my mother, the decorator, said. "I think you'll be very comfy."

I was more than *comfy* in their guest room, which was practically larger than my entire apartment. Mom had decorated it with soft peaches and teals down to the shower cap in my private bathroom. Marac had made himself at home on the cushioned wicker chair next to my bed.

"Mom," I said that evening after dinner, "your trailer is unbelievably spacious. I'm going to feel claustrophobic when I go back to my Brooklyn digs."

"Brooke, please," said my mother, always politically correct, "it's called a manufactured home these days, but

I'm glad you like it. Dad and I are very happy here…we're having a second honeymoon."

"When did the first one stop?" Dad said.

That night, while getting ready for bed, I realized that my marriage to Kyle had been far from ideal. After I got over the sting of our separation, I admitted my parents had been right when they asked us to wait until we knew each other a little better. Of course, I didn't listen to them, nor did Kyle take his widowed father's similar advice, and we shamelessly ignored the pre-marital counseling our church offered. I guess that's when I stopped attending services. Kyle and I were fresh out of college ready to have it all: the perfect marriage with a perfect apartment, and eventually two perfect little kids. So much for perfection.

Maybe a change of scenery was what I needed to start over. With Marac tightly curled up against me and softly purring, I slept a solid ten hours.

My parents left on Friday, two days after I arrived, leaving me with Marac and written lists should I need anything from papayas to light bulbs, plus the number for the local hair salon. Mom had dropped a not-so-subtle hint that a few blond highlights might brighten up my winter-dull hair.

"And don't forget the most important thing. Jesse, the handyman, lives at 135 Pine Lane, and he knows how to fix everything. His number is right by the phone. Now be sure to close the first door before opening the second one or Marac will run for his life," Dad said.

"I'll be fine. You go off to see the Queen. Marac and I will be right here when you get back," I said, petting my furry companion who had woven himself around my legs.

After my parents left with their travel mates, I sipped a

second cup of coffee and planned the rest of my day. I went for a quick swim, and since Mom had stocked the fridge with dinner provisions, I decided to walk over to Brandy's, the local market, for some cake ingredients. When I returned, I was careful to close the outer door before opening the inner one.

All of a sudden the first door swung open, and Marac escaped.

Startled, I dropped the groceries on the floor and heard the bottle of lime juice smash to smithereens right before a dozen eggs splattered into the gooey mess. There goes the Key Lime Layer Cake. I knew it would be a nightmare to clean up, but my first priority was to get Marac back in the house.

I scoured the narrow streets of Sandy Shores searching for the fugitive, but there was no sign of him in between the neatly lined-up homes. While hunting for Marac, I noticed how attractively all the residents kept their property. There were window boxes filled with hot pink impatiens and cheery red begonias, stone walkways, colorful front doors and bright curtains visible from the street. Without realizing it, I arrived at 135 Pine Lane and there on the front porch sat Marac, sunning himself. Next to a Great Dane.

The cat treats I'd brought along didn't tempt Marac to leave his spot. I gingerly approached the twosome and tried to scare away the gigantic, intimidating-looking dog. I stomped my feet, waved my arms, and yelled something like "bugga bugga" but the Dane didn't budge. If cats could laugh, Marac would have done so right in my face.

"That's some pretty fancy singing and dancing," a deep masculine voice called out to me.

A young man exited the front door of the mobile home at 135 Pine Lane and smiled. He was wearing tattered overalls and a T-shirt, plus a low-slung tool belt.

Enter Jesse the handyman.

I was too exhausted from my feline pursuit to be embarrassed, so decided to play along with him.

"Yes, it's the latest craze in New York."

"Oh, then you must be Brooke. I'm Jesse. Your parents told me you'd be staying at their place for the next couple of weeks. Anything wrong?"

"Not exactly, but somehow Marac ran away, and I've been chasing him down all over Sandy Shores till I found him here a minute ago. I was sure I'd closed the doors correctly, but Houdini here got out anyway," I said.

"I'm not surprised to hear that. I told your mom that the outer door wasn't working properly and that I needed to make an adjustment, but she said it could wait until they returned from their trip. I thought that was chancy because Marac will run over here any chance he gets to sit with old Pluto, not that we mind his company. They're BFF, as the kids say. Oh, don't be afraid of him. He's big, but friendly and seriously lazy. Now I'm kind of glad that I didn't get around to repairing that door. It's nice to meet you," Jesse said.

So that was it. As a side dish to her trip to England, Mom had wanted me to meet Jesse without a formal fix-up, which she knew I'd never go for. Marac's break-out was the ideal solution. From past experience, she'd be sure that he and I would both end up at Jesse's.

"Nice to meet you, too," I said.

"I hear you're a food writer, Brooke. That sounds like fun."

"It used to be. Now it's just a twenty-four seven job. I've been trying to write my own cookbook for ages, but never seem to have the time, so that's what I'll be working on while I'm here. And Mom promised the chaplain that I'd make an appearance at the church luncheon with a home-made cake. Seems I can't show up empty handed," I said, making a mental note to return to Brandy's.

"Well then, I may have to show up myself. Frankly, I don't know why I got away from going to services, but now I have a reason to make it this Sunday. I'll even dress up for the occasion. I can meet you at your place on Sunday, fix the door, and then we can walk over to the church. Sound good?" he said.

"Jesse, can I be honest with you? I haven't been to church in well over a year because my job is so stressful that I need the extra sleep on Sundays. Thanks for not making me feel guilty," I said, giggling a bit.

I am not a giggler.

"Whew, that makes me feel better. Thought I'd get a lecture from you. Now I can't wait for Sunday," he said, with a welcoming smile.

"You don't have to wait until Sunday. Why don't you join me for dinner tonight?" I said, wondering if I had enough time to schedule some highlights at the salon.

My boldness surprised me, but there was something so sincere about Jesse's smile that I felt completely at ease with him, plus he already had my parents' stamp of approval.

"Sure," said Jesse, "and don't worry about Marac. I'll bring him along with me. Uh, Brooke, maybe if we have time later, think you could teach me some of those dance steps?"

"Absolutely. Wait a minute. Did you seriously name your seriously lazy dog Pluto?"

"Yeah, it suits him, don't you think?" he said.

"It's perfect," I said, giving new meaning to the word.

FREE SPIRITS

Katherine sat in one of the rickety ladder-back chairs that she'd pulled out from under the wooden dining table. The table was scarred after years of neglect from renters not putting down trivets for hot coffee carafes, or even from those who might have crushed out a cigarette or two, or let a candle burn too long. The sign about no smoking in the cabin went unheeded. There were also the honeymoon couples who'd carved their initials into the hard, maple tabletop like she and Wyatt had done.

She thought about their beautiful wedding day with Adrienne and Louise as her two maids of honor. They were each so dear to her she couldn't choose one over the other. Since it was a summer wedding, the girls had worn strapless,

pale green gowns with matching shawls for the church ceremony and then danced the night away, their wraps and satin
sandals tossed aside. Katherine's wedding dress had been her
late mother's. Her father gave her away and there were tears
in his eyes as he pulled back his daughter's veil. It was a perfect day that continued into the wee hours of the morning
with a fun-filled reception, and a raucous after-party for the
bride and groom, their attendants and friends. She and Wyatt fell into bed too exhausted to make love. There would be
plenty of time for that in the following years, the years that
never happened for them.

She waited for him now as she'd done in the past on the
exact date of what would have been their fifth anniversary,
and he'd never disappointed her. Would he still care enough
to come five years after their honeymoon, which began so
joyously but ended in tragedy?

"Katherine, you're here," Wyatt said, almost like a question as he walked into the cottage.

"Happy anniversary, darling. Of course I'm here. I've
been waiting for you, but only a short while." She paused,
not wanted to bring up any negativity on their only day
together. "I was wondering if you'd come back this year,"
she said.

"Yes, Katherine, I'm here for you," Wyatt said. "Funny
thing is I wasn't sure if you'd return."

"How could I not? It would have been our fifth. We're
always together for our anniversary. Remember how shocked
we were that first year? That you could actually see me?"

"That's true, of course I remember, but I didn't know if
it'd be the same this time," he said without smiling. "Things
change, Katherine."

"Not my love for you," she said. "Or this old summer
house. Look, our initials are still here. I guess the owners
must have a soft spot for lovers because they've never sanded

down the table. I always think back to our honeymoon. Remember?"

"Who could forget? We thought we'd be totally alone, then all those fishermen passing by the cottage every morning on their way to the dock," he said. "Remember that guy who poked his head through the window to ask if we had any coffee made yet? It's a good thing we were up and dressed for our swim."

"But even with that it was wonderful, what little time we had together. A week before the accident. It went by so quickly," Katherine said, as she traced their initials with a slender finger.

"Yes, it was blissful until the drowning took us away from each other. I've never forgiven myself for that. It shouldn't have happened," he said.

"It wasn't your fault, darling. No one could have helped."

"I should have seen it coming—been more aware of the riptides," Wyatt said. "But, that was five years ago. The accident is in the past where it belongs."

"You're right, sweetheart. Let's not talk about it. We usually only have a few hours together and I want to talk about us, and our lives together.

"You were the love of my life, but our life together is over. It was over five years ago after the accident. I've accepted it, and you will have to also or neither of us will ever be at peace," Wyatt said, a little more sternly.

"Our life as we knew it is over, but at least we have our anniversary, the one day we're somehow able to share."

"Katherine, we have to talk about that. Coming here each year."

"It's not a problem, is it? We both manage."

"It's not a question of managing. It's a question of moving on," he said.

"I don't understand. I thought this was as important to you as it is to me."

"Let me try to help you. After the accident, the drowning, when we were separated, I never thought I'd see you again. Then on our first anniversary I decided to come here just to be in the spot where we were so much in love. The last thing I ever expected was to see you. It was a miracle. I never thought that would be possible," he said.

"One of the great mysteries of life after death, right?" Katherine said.

Wyatt paced while gathering his thoughts. He had to make his wife understand why he wanted to stop meeting with her year after year.

"That's what we need to talk about. Life, not death," he said.

Katherine, who'd gotten up from the table to move toward him, had her own thoughts. She would not allow their anniversary to go unobserved. This one day was enough to carry her through until the following year.

"What we need is to come here every year, like we've been doing for the past five. It's the only time we can be together and talk about what..." she said, her words beginning to falter.

"Darling, we talk about what might have been. We can't go back in time. You have to know that."

"Have you stopped loving me?" she asked, a feeling of weakness overtaking her.

"I'll never stop loving you. You'll always be in my heart, but even our marriage vows said till death do us part.'"

"I'll never forget our vows. You were the only man for me then, and now. Childhood sweethearts. Always being there for each other. That can't and shouldn't stop just because the accident ended our beautiful life together."

"Katherine, please listen to me. No one could have

predicted the drowning that day, least of all me. I was a strong swimmer, but the current was stronger. I tried to reach you but I couldn't make it in time. I know it's trite, but there's a whole world out there, yes, a different world from what we had, and there has to be something for each of us," Wyatt said.

"Maybe for you, but remember, we'd only been married for two weeks. We never even celebrated our first anniversary. That's why I came here five years ago, to see if you remembered and you did. Darling, we found each other again, if only for one day a year. It ties us together. Why would you want to break that apart?" she said.

"What ties us together is weakening, and it will pull us apart. I know you must realize it too."

Katherine felt more fragile than ever, but she wouldn't allow herself to agree with what Wyatt was telling her. She would try to stay strong although her energy was beginning to wane. "I don't want it to weaken. I want us to meet each year. Please say you will. Is it difficult for you to get here?" she asked, almost as an afterthought.

"It's not that. I'll come for as long as you need me to, but please think about what I've said. You'll never be at peace if you don't accept death. Neither of us will be."

"Wyatt, even if you're right it's still the one day I'm able to look forward to. There's nothing else for me. Is there for you?" she asked.

"I don't know. As long as you still want to return, I'll never find out. I won't desert you, but is there really nothing out there for you?" he said.

"You want to be free, is that it?" she said.

"I think it's the right thing, for both of us."

Wyatt's tone softened as he tried to explain his feelings. He couldn't let Katherine be tortured year after year wondering if they would ever see each other again.

"Sweetheart, what do you think? Do you agree?" he asked.

"I don't want to think about it…putting an end to all this," she said, opening her arms as if to embrace the cottage.

"All what? This place is falling down around us. It'll probably be sold or rebuilt sooner or later, and we wouldn't be able to meet here anyway. You're putting too much pressure on yourself," Wyatt said, trying to be pragmatic. "And the past."

"It's the one place where we were together. I can't let them tear it down," Katherine said, her voice growing softer and less forceful.

"Oh, you certainly won't have any say in that matter. We never owned it. We only rented it that one time for our honeymoon."

"I'll go anywhere you say. It'll never be a problem for me," she said.

"You're not listening. Please make this the last time and end it today," he said.

Now Katherine's voice was barely above a whisper. Everything would be lost to her if Wyatt didn't want to return.

"I don't know what will happen to me if I don't have this day to look forward to. Time has no meaning anymore," she said.

"I don't know what the future will hold for either of us, but I know we can't dwell in the past anymore. There is a future for each of us, but it's just not together," he said.

"But without the past I won't be able to feel anything at all. It's like I'm the one who…" she murmured, before Wyatt broke in.

"I know what you're going to say! You feel like you're the one who died, but you're not. I'm the one who drowned five years ago. You have to stop thinking that the accident ended your life. You still have a life. It was me who died. I tried to swim to you in time, but I couldn't make it. I saw you there, standing on the shore waving me in, God knows, I tried. Katherine, you're the one who's alive. You must learn to live. You have to let go, for both our sakes," he said.

"But if I let go how will I know what will happen to you?"

Wyatt laughed and started to fade from sight.

"It's like you said. The living will never understand everything about death. You'll find out in your own way, I'd say fifty or sixty years from now. I want you to find love again. It will happen if you let it. And I must be set free to rest in peace. That would be the best anniversary present you could give to me, and to yourself," he said, drifting away.

"Yes, I'll do that for you," she said.

"And for yourself," he repeated. "Promise me that."

"I promise," she said, her last words to Wyatt before he vanished. Then aloud in a stronger tone she said, "I'll drive back into town now. Maybe I'll call Adrienne and Louise to meet me for dinner. I'll start over."

Katherine pushed the chair back under the ancient wood table and gazed one last time around the cottage where she'd shared a wonderful time with Wyatt. It would always be a precious memory, but it would no longer stop her from going on with her life.

THE ICING
ON THE CAKE

"The wedding's off," my mother says, hanging up the phone in our family's bakery the second I walk through the front door. "Brian feels he's not ready. He says you can leave the ring at his mother's. The diamond belongs in their family."

That's how my day begins.

"But we're engaged! Today is Friday and the wedding's Saturday," I say, gasping for breath. "You're making the cake today! This can't be happening! I've already had my bachelorette party and the girls all got mani-pedis! What about our hair? The flowers? My dress! Aunt Natalie made my dress! Why didn't he call me? Didn't he even want to speak to me?" I say, feeling my heart begin to thump like a jackhammer. I don't bother putting my questions in order because nothing has sunk in yet. Oh, and you could say I'm frantic and totally losing it.

"Jenna, not only is it happening, but I'm glad about it. Your father will be too once he hears the news," Mom says. "Brian said he felt bad enough without telling you himself."

"He feels bad?" I say, trying to subdue my inner shriek. "How can he do this to me? What are we going to do? The wedding is tomorrow, in case you forgot. We have a hundred guests coming. Wait a minute. The rehearsal dinner is tonight at Brian's house."

"Calm yourself, sweetie. Everything will be taken care of," my mother says, sounding like a Mafia hit man or hit woman, or whatever.

My parents never thought Brian and I were well matched, and my mom has reminded me of that fact approximately three times a day for the year that we've been dating. Although Brian and I didn't exactly see eye to eye on several matters, we still decided to become engaged and work things out as we went along. I'm wearing the ring he gave me. The one he wants returned because he's not marrying me tomorrow, and I'm crying my eyes out.

I slump down at the counter with my head perched between open palms as my elbows straddle one of the jumbo bowls of cake ingredients, and I begin to shed a fresh batch of tears into the shiny yellow mixture.

"Stop crying, dear," my mother says, "you'll ruin the batter."

"You're not still making a wedding cake. There's no wedding," I say, trying not to screech again.

"Aunt Natalie's due here soon, and we'll get organized with phone calls and anything else that needs to be done. It's not the disaster you think it is," Mom says. "It's a bump in the road."

I've just received the worst news of my life, yet my mother doesn't think it's a disaster. Only a little glitch, according to her. How nice. I'm ready to spill out the batter when, with one look, Mom silently cautions me against doing so.

"We're all going to make cupcakes," she says.

My mother announces this like she's planning a Girl Scout picnic.

"Mom, you can't think that selling cupcakes made out of my wedding cake batter is a good idea. That has to be bad luck for everyone." I break down in yet another set of sobs. "Brian is dumping me and you're baking mini-reminders of the biggest humiliation of my life. Of course, it's a disaster."

"You'll get over it, and I don't mind saying I think Brian did you a favor. His timing wasn't great, but Dad and I never thought he was the right man for you, and you would have come to the same conclusion sooner or later. Better that it's sooner," says my mother, who obviously doesn't mind saying it at all.

Aunt Natalie comes through the door that very minute, her usual cheery self. Boy, is she in the wrong place today.

"Hi, everyone. Let's get to work on that cake. Uh oh, what is it? Jenna, honey, what's wrong?" Aunt Natalie says.

"I didn't have time to call you," Mom says to her sister, "and I knew you were on your way. Jenna has something to tell you."

I give Aunt Natalie the *Reader's Digest* version of the break-up.

"Aw, Jenna, don't cry. We can still have a party. All that food, it would be a sin to waste it," says my beloved aunt.

"No, Aunt Natalie, I refuse to celebrate anything tomorrow. Maybe I'll feel better in a year from now, or never, but please don't ask me to come to any party on what was supposed to be my wedding day," I say, as she wraps her arms around me. Aunt Natalie has always championed my causes and the most important one, at least for today, is that she and Uncle Russell adored Brian.

"Honey, if I may say so, you're better off without him. Uncle Russell and I never thought he was right for you," Aunt Natalie says, releasing me from her embrace.

I'm now living in a parallel universe where people say things that are in direct opposition to what they previously said, or vice versa.

"*Et tu*, Aunt Natalie?" I say.

"Come on now. Brian's not a bad guy, we just…" Mom begins.

"Yes Mother, I know. I'm better off without him."

"What are we going to do with all the food we made?" Aunt Natalie says, mainly to break up the tension because it'll be a cold day you know where when my mother doesn't have a Plan B.

On cue Mom says, "Let's donate most of the food and the cupcakes to The Lord's Place. Brady runs the shelter and he's sure to be there today. He'll be thrilled to have the extra dessert. How's that, sweetheart?"

My parents bring their leftover cakes, breads, and pies to the food shelter several times a week. It's on their way home from the bakery, and sometimes she and my dad stay to help serve.

"Jenna, all you have to do after we bake the cupcakes is to box them up and take them over to Brady's. Dad will prepare the food to go, and I'll call over to the shelter to say that you have a big drop off," Mom says, and throws an apron to me.

Aunt Natalie, Mom, and I bake for several hours while my dad makes phone calls. He's totally cool about it and tells the guests that the rehearsal dinner and wedding are off, and doesn't offer an explanation. All the gifts will be returned. He cancels the ceremony at the church and tells the priest to enjoy the flowers that have already arrived. He calls Janie Franklin, my maid of honor with freshly French-manicured nails, and gives her the news. Janie will notify the other bridesmaids, and Dad assumes that Brian will take care of the groomsmen. Since Aunt Natalie made all the bridal party dresses, which was to be her gift to me, at least the girls won't be out too much money.

Dad calls our wedding planner, Adam Goode, who insists upon handling everything else, including Daisy's Gazebo, where our reception is scheduled. It was one of the few venues that allowed outside catering, which my mom had insisted upon. She and Aunt Natalie are major cooks, and I'm sure our hundred plus guests were looking forward to being well fed.

Adam's also been working with a couple who are celebrating their fiftieth anniversary by renewing their vows. Their friends and family had been invited to the ceremony, and now they'll have a spacious new place for a reception instead of a crowded living room. Adam's on speaker, so I hear exactly how he's going to figure out the replacement event.

"You know, the room is paid for and they won't issue a refund at this late date. Might as well let these folks have it. Pay it forward and all that," Adam says. "They already have the food ordered and I'll make sure it gets delivered to Daisy's. Sorry, Jenna, I know you must feel like you've been hit by a truck, but you know what they say: when one door closes, another one opens, or a window, or something like that," he says.

Or it stays shut.

"Thanks, Adam. I'd glad you're able to arrange everything. I'll let you talk to Dad. I have to help Mom and my aunt," I say, while sniffling and picking away at my own manicured hands.

The beautiful room where Brian and I were supposed to have our first dance as a married couple is now going to Mr. and Mrs. Fifty Years Together. I hope they enjoy the centerpieces.

"Dad, you're the best," I say, after he's off the phone. I have to give him credit because he doesn't remind me that he never much cared for Brian in the first place. Mom can't help herself, so I tune her out while I get ready to frost the cupcakes.

"I let your mom think she runs the business, but I'm the organization man," he says, and I finally get in a good laugh.

"How will I know which one Brady is?" I ask, while spreading the French vanilla icing before adding a squiggle of pistachio cream topping.

I'm enjoying the work although I certainly can't admit that to Mom. She and Dad still want me to come into the bakery business, but I prefer my job as a room planner for a large furniture store. I'll have my official degree as a professional interior designer in a few months, but in the meanwhile I've gotten some serious on-the-job training, and that's also how I met Brian, who'd recently moved into a condo and needed to furnish it. After the initial consult, and some copies of room layouts, he asked if I were allowed to date clients. I was, and we did.

Dorothy Lane, my boss, had given me a few days off so I could relax and prepare for the wedding. Dorothy was all business, but nobody is really happy when a wedding is called off. The silver lining for Dorothy would be that I might be available to work over the weekend, the most popular time for shoppers.

"Jenna, are you listening to me? You asked me about Brady. He's an elderly gentleman with a white beard and wears big thick glasses. He's a little hard of hearing, so you may have to ring three or four times. He should be expecting you. Brady's always there on Fridays because that's the biggest day at the shelter. It wouldn't hurt you to lend them a hand once in a while," Mom says.

"Mom, please let me recover from Brian, then, I guess you're right. I'll see about helping out a day or two after work. Maybe it'll take my mind off becoming an old maid."

"Pshaw! You're only twenty-three. You have lots of time," says Aunt Natalie, who eloped with Uncle Russell forty years ago when she was eighteen.

"Your aunt is right. Now stop wasting time thinking about your ex-fiancé, and get on with your life. Why don't you give me the ring? I'll return it for you. That wasn't fair of Brian to ask you to do it. Speaks volumes about his character," Mom lectures on.

"Mom, please! Drop it!"

I've been a hysteric all morning, so decide to lighten up and add a little comic relief to the conversation. "Speaking of dropping things, do you think you could drop the ring into the batter and let someone at the shelter get the lucky cupcake?"

Later that afternoon all the food and cupcakes are ready to go and loaded into my dad's van. I've calmed down somewhat, but it's more likely that I'm in shock now that the news has finally sunk in.

"Do you want me to drive you over there, sweetie?" Dad says.

"No," Mom says. "It's better if she goes by herself. There's enough help at the shelter to unload. I need you at the store today because the Bradfords called in an order for a batch of whole wheat biscuits."

"They did? Hmm, I guess they didn't know about the…" Dad says, stopping short of mentioning the dreaded wedding word.

"Okay, Jenna, here are the keys. If you have any problems, give me a call. Got your cell with you?" says my concerned father.

"Sure, Dad. It's attached to my hip."

"No texting while you're driving," he cautions, like I haven't heard that before.

"Only when I'm speeding," I counter, knowing he doesn't take me seriously.

Fifteen minutes later I'm at the shelter awkwardly clutching a box of cupcakes in one arm as I ring the back doorbell with my free hand. I remember what Mom said about Brady being hard of hearing, so I press the bell a few more times.

"Hold your horses, I'm on my way," says a man with a strong voice. Doesn't sound much like the senior citizen Mom made Brady out to be.

I reposition the box of cupcakes just as a tall man about my age wearing a starched white apron over khakis, a knit shirt, and a smile, opens the door. He doesn't have a white beard or any kind of glasses. His hair is jet black, and his eyes are the color of Mom's Double-Fudge Filling. Obviously it's not Brady, and I hope I'm not staring too hard because this guy is so good-looking that I could easily make a fool out of myself, but then I remember that I'd already accomplished that with Brian.

"Thanks for coming, Jenna," he says, taking the lead. "Your mom told me you were on your way."

"But you're not Brady," I say, stumbling over my words as I come up with this clever observation.

"Brady's my grandfather," he says, looking a little confused. "My name's Jared. Jenna, please don't be embarrassed, but your mom mentioned the break-up. Sorry to hear about it. Why don't you try to think about all the good you'll be doing by donating the food and these cupcakes, which are going to be an extra-special hit," he says, as I blush the same shade as our Red Velvet Layer Cake. "When things aren't meant to be, it's better to find out early in the game. I've been there. How about some coffee?"

"Thanks, that'd be great," I say, as he takes the heavy box from my outstretched arms.

"Come on in and I'll show you around," he says.

I look through the door, which is wide open, and Adam's words come back to me. I decide to go for it.

"If you're short-handed, I could stay and help serve now that my weekend is free," I say, deciding Dorothy can live without me for the few days I was supposed to have off anyway.

"Thanks," he says, his chocolaty eyes lighting up. "I can always use a little extra help."

"Is your grandfather here?" I say, once we move into the shelter's kitchen. "Mom wanted me to say hi."

Jared throws back his head and roars with laughter.

"What's so funny?" I say.

"Brady never works on Fridays. That's his fishing day with the guys. I can't believe your mom played the grandfather card."

I'll deal with Mom tonight, but right now Jared's upbeat personality is getting to me, and I know sooner or later I'll have to get over the drama with my ex.

"If you don't mind, I'd rather not discuss my broken engagement," I say.

"That'll work," he says. "Why don't we talk about these cupcakes and sample a few?"

I'm about to balk about eating the seeds of treachery, but it's only cake. They no longer represent a relationship that almost led down the wrong path.

"Sure. Mom's recipe is the best," I say.

It turns out that Mom and Aunt Natalie were right after all because a year later Dad walked me down the aisle and Brady was Jared's best man. Mom baked the cake, and I wore a new bridal gown that Aunt Natalie insisted upon making, along with the bridesmaids' dresses. (She'd donated the previous bridal wardrobe to a local consignment shop without mentioning the history.)

When Jared and I entered the reception hall at Daisy's Gazebo as husband and wife for the first time, I saw the centerpieces that Adam had been keeping a secret. Low-cut white roses surrounding a hand-painted miniature wooden door graced each of the twelve tables.

ACT ONE

"Thank you for another delicious dinner, Mom," Candy said.

"You're welcome, dear," said her mother, Cynthia, "and don't forget to take the leftovers home with you. Oh, I almost forgot. There's a half-gallon of Rocky Road in the freezer. I bought it by mistake."

"Mom, even with three Emmys sitting on the mantle you can't pull that off. You bought the ice cream for me because you know it's my favorite. My reward for working late?"

"You could call it that, but you're as thin as a rail and I know you don't like to shop or cook."

"Mom, I don't have much extra time and I don't want to

spend it in the supermarket. But thanks anyway, I've always wanted to be a thin rail," Candy said, knowing she could get a rise out of her sophisticated mother.

"Oh, joke about it all you like, but it seems all you do lately is work. And Candace, I don't have to remind you that you haven't had one date since starting at the paper," Cynthia said with a *tsk*.

"No," Candy said, trying not to laugh, "I don't have to be reminded, but I'm sure you'll do it anyway."

As the entertainment editor of the local newspaper, Candy had to admit, if only to herself, that it would be a nice change to have a man escort her to the plays and music events she was required to review as part of her job. She enjoyed dressing up when attending a show, usually wearing the outfits that her mother, who had impeccable taste, had purchased for her. When Cynthia first began the routine of shopping for her daughter, Candy was annoyed and said she wasn't nine years old anymore and was quite capable of picking out her own clothing. Cynthia persisted and because Candy's time was so limited, she realized it was a dual blessing. It helped fill her widowed mother's days, and Candy had a fabulous wardrobe.

"Now, don't get angry at me, but I've signed you up for an acting course at the Fortune Theater. Grace told me about it because Matthew will be taking the class also. If you're reviewing theater, you might as well have a full understanding of it, including the actors' point of view," Cynthia said.

"Mom, you go to half the shows with me and I get your feedback. Honestly, I wish you'd discussed this course with me first. I can't stand Matthew. He's so conceited," Candy said, groaning inwardly.

"As you are well aware, Matthew is my godchild and

he happens to be very good-looking. Grace and Howard do spoil him, but at least he has something to be conceited about. And he's an only child, like you."

"Hey, that's not my fault. I always wanted a brother or sister, and the way you and Dad were always kissing, I thought it was in the bag," Candy said.

"Now don't you be fresh to your mother," Cynthia said, not really meaning it.

Cynthia paused for a moment and filled her stemmed goblet halfway with a rich Cabernet. She sat on the deep comfortable living room sofa and patted the cushion next to her.

"Let's have a little talk," Cynthia said.

"What is it, Mom? Are you okay?" Candy said, arranging herself on the chaise portion of the wraparound sofa.

"I'm fine. I thought maybe it's time to explain why you're an only child. Since Dad died you've become my closest confidant, beside Grace, so here goes. We did want more children, but after you were born we were still struggling financially and it would have been impossible. As it was, Dad and I used to take you to rehearsals, and you can thank Grace for looking after you backstage. By the time we were making a good living, I was in my early thirties and felt a little too old to start with another baby, but we tried anyway. After two miscarriages the doctor warned against any further pregnancies," Cynthia said.

"Oh, Mom, I'm so sorry. I never knew," Candy said, putting her arm around her mother's shoulders. "You and Dad did so much for me. It must have bothered you when I bugged you for a little sister or brother."

"No, not really. All kids do that, I think, except maybe Matthew. He's happy being top gun in that family," Cynthia said, making them both laugh. "It's different in today's world. Women have babies all the way into their late forties, but I don't think you should wait that long."

"Me? I'm not dating anyone, so let's not talk about babies just yet," Candy said.

Cynthia rose from the sofa to perch on the curved arm of a large club chair.

"Uh oh, I see you've shifted over to your podium. Let's have it," Candy said.

"If you could only carry on our family tradition by becoming an actress, that would be my fondest dream. And imagine if you and Matthew hit it off! I know he's self-absorbed, but he's does quite well in the brokerage business, and Grace and I would plan a beautiful wedding. The children of two lifelong friends finally getting married! It's what your father would have wanted," Cynthia said, in her most dramatic voice.

"Hold it right there, Meryl Streep. Dad always told me that I had my choice of careers and to be sure to marry for love, like you guys did. I'm a journalist and I know right now it's only for theater and stuff, but that has value. One day I'd like to take on bigger projects, but I have to work my way up the ladder. The paper's been good to me, and I enjoy what I do," Candy said in defense of her profession. "And before you and Grace start decorating the church, Matthew and I are not about to become the next big husband and wife team, like you and Dad."

Candy's father, Kevin Conrad, best known for his role as Professor LaGrange on a popular daytime drama called *Our Brightest Days*, had fallen in love with Cynthia after she was cast as Emily Kimberly, the school superintendent. They appeared together for thirty years until a heart attack had forced her dad to retire from the show. Six weeks later he passed away and Cynthia left shortly thereafter. Candy missed him terribly, and helped fill her mother's lonely evenings by sharing a home-cooked meal with her at least once a week. Candy had always been closer to her dad, but spending more time with her mother had brought about a new connection between the two women.

Grace and her husband, Howard, made sure Cynthia and Candy were invited to Sunday dinners since Kevin's passing, and they were grateful for their extended family and support system, even if it meant listening to Matthew hold court at the weekend meal.

"Please indulge me and try that acting class. Grace was all puffed up like a peacock at our Bible study group last week bragging about her soon-to-be celebrity son. I couldn't let her hang that over me, so I said you'd signed up for the same course and wasn't that just peachy!"

"Oh, so it's the big Grace/Cynthia competition for a change. I thought you two were best buddies," Candy said.

"Of course, we're best friends. Have been since we met on the show, but she's always been a little jealous of my success. Grace couldn't act to save her life, but she knew her way around making the sets look good—I'll give her that—and now she's trying to one-up me and I don't much like it."

"Please remember that you two may be best friends, but you'll never be in-laws," Candy said, continuing to push her mother's buttons.

"All right, I won't press the issue," Cynthia said, backing down, "but you do need to get out more and socialize. Besides, it's my treat and I've already paid for it. It's simply an offer you can't refuse."

Candy started to protest again, but Cynthia was already on her way to the kitchen.

"Okay, Don Corleone, I accept the offer," Candy called out to her mother. "I'll give it a shot."

"You'll love the classes," Cynthia said, filling an oversized shopping bag with enough food for a week. "They start this Monday evening at seven. And why don't you get to know Matthew a little better; you never can tell."

"I've known that legend-in-his-own-mind since kindergarten and he was a pain in the butt back then, but I promise to be civil. Maybe the class will be fun after all, provided I don't have to kiss Matthew on or off stage," Candy said.

"I can't hear you! I'm getting the Rocky Road out of the freezer," Cynthia said. "And don't say butt."

While Candy drove to the theater the following week, she began to regret accepting her mother's gift. She'd have to put up with Matthew, who probably fancied himself as the next Bradley Cooper, and there would most likely be some old washed up has-been for a teacher. Not wanting to disappoint her mother, Candy decided to give the course a fair chance. After all, acting was in her genes if not exactly in her blood. And maybe Matthew wouldn't be so bad in a group setting.

As soon as she parked her car she heard someone call out, "Candace! Over here. Hurry up, so we can go inside together." It had to be Matthew. He was the only person other than her mother who used her given name. One look at him preening in front of the glass door reminded Candy of how self-centered he'd always been.

Too bad those great looks with the perfect hair are wasted on a dud, she thought.

"I have to get my notebook out of the trunk. I'll be right there. You go on in," she said, lagging behind so no one thought they were a couple.

Candy grabbed her tote bag and waited a few minutes before entering the theater. After she signed in, Candy walked over to Matthew, who was in conversation with a tall, rugged-looking man, casually dressed in jeans and a chambray work shirt. Matthew had shown up in his Sunday best.

"You're just in time; we're about to start. Hal, meet Candace," Matthew said. "He's going…"

"How do you do," she said, interrupting Matthew's introduction. "Hal, I guess you're another aspiring actor, like my friend Matthew," she said, stressing the word friend.

Candy shook Hal's hand, and felt a slight electric shock. *Must be the carpet in the lobby,* she thought.

"Well, sort of. It's nice to meet you. I didn't realize there would be so many people interested in this class," Hal said, with a smile that crinkled up his gorgeous, ocean-blue eyes.

"Hopefully we'll get a decent teacher, but I wouldn't count on it," said Candy.

"Candace, I was about to say…" Matthew broke in.

"What's his name, anyway? I should have looked at the roster. My mom signed me up so I never saw the application," she rambled on, somewhat aware that she'd been rude to Matthew.

"The teacher's name is Harrison Rhodes, and from what I've heard he's a real drill sergeant," Hal said. "We better get in there before he comes out with a whip and a chair looking for us."

Ten other students joined them in the theater, but the teacher had yet to appear.

"Where is this guy, anyway?" Candy said to Hal, "I don't understand why he's late."

"Okay, I'd better come clean," he said, turning to the group.

"Hi, everyone," he said, "my name's Harrison Rhodes, but everyone calls me Hal. I'll be your acting teacher for the next eight weeks."

"If you had let me finish a sentence, you wouldn't have made a fool out of yourself," Matthew hissed at Candy.

Candy felt her face redden after hearing Hal reveal his identity, but his smile put her at ease.

"Sorry," she whispered to Matthew.

"As long as we're an even number, I'll break you up into pairs, and it would be a good idea if you could get together during the week to rehearse on your own," Hal continued. "We'll discuss a few scenes before you read them, but first let's try a little improvisation or 'improv' as we call it in the business. That'll loosen you up, and get rid of those inhibitions. Feel free to be as creative as you like. This is where it all begins. I'll leave it up to you to invent a story, but if anyone needs a prompt, I have a few written down on the board."

Candy prayed that Hal wouldn't match her up with Matthew, but her pleas went unanswered when the instructor called out their names as one of the twosomes. Somehow, she'd have to try to withstand Matthew's insufferable ego while in class.

After their first few minutes of improv, Candy realized she didn't have much to worry about. Matthew had taken the upper hand in the play-acting, and she barely squeezed in a line. Matthew did surprisingly well in the situation that he'd invented: strangers meeting in the park, each on their way to a secretive meeting. Candy did her best to match Matthew's energy and nuances, but she knew her performance was sorely lacking in both areas.

"Well done, all," Hal said, after everyone had finished. "Now that you're relaxed, I'd like you to read aloud the scenes I've prepared before we call it quits for tonight. The improv was amazing. I can't believe you guys have never acted before."

The class broke up at hearing Hal's exaggerated accolades

because they knew, aside from Matthew's performance, how comical some of their attempts had been. Matthew received much praise from the class, and even Hal mentioned his natural ability. Matthew modestly accepted the well-deserved honors, and Candy felt a little guilty about how inconsiderate she'd been earlier in the evening.

Hal handed out their scene assignments, and led them through some vocal exercises and a series of stretches he said many actors used before a performance. He made sure that each member of the class received individual attention so that even the shyest of the would-be actors began to feel comfortable.

"Okay, guys, just read the first few pages so everyone has a chance tonight. Next week, after you've had time to go over the scene, you can read or act it out," Hal said. "Some of you will be able to commit your lines to memory, but don't worry if you can't. That takes practice. Candy and Matthew, why don't you start us off?"

The script that Hal gave to them was a thriller. Matthew was to play a detective conducting an investigation of a recent murder that had taken place in a butcher shop. Candy's role was that of a customer who had witnessed the alleged suspect running out the side door. The rest of the class followed them until everyone had the opportunity to read. Candy was intrigued by the quality of the scripts and scratched down a note to ask Hal about them. Some were love stories, others mysteries like the one she and Matthew read, but they were all extremely well written.

"Candace," Matthew said at the end of the class, "let's go out for a cup of coffee. I want to dig right into our scene. You've got a lot of work to do. I'd be glad to give you notes."

"Not tonight, Lieutenant Columbo, I have to be at the office very early in the morning," Candy said, trying her best to be amenable. "How about if we meet after work tomorrow evening?"

"Sure, we can discuss our parts over dinner. Dutch treat, of course," he said.

"Of course," Candy answered with false cheer.

Candy waited until the rest of the group left the theater before approaching her teacher.

"Hal, the class was incredible. I really enjoyed it and you're certainly not what I expected for a teacher. If you have a minute, I wanted to ask you something about the scripts."

"Sure, Candy, or do you prefer Candace?" Hal asked.

"Candy. Only Matthew and my mother call me Candace. Mom thinks I'm going to become a famous actress one day like she was, but not with a name like Candy. Her name is Cynthia, but she'd kill anyone who'd dare call her Cindy."

"Wait a minute, there's only one famous Cynthia I've ever heard of. Don't tell me you're talking about Cynthia Conrad?" he said.

"Sure am," Candy said, taking a bow.

"Then that makes you Candy Conrad, local theater expert. I read your column all the time. I'm honored you're in my class," he said, returning the bow. "What did you want to ask me?"

She wanted to ask Hal how his eyes could be so insanely blue, but instead said, "I was wondering who wrote tonight's material. Everything was quite professional yet none of it seemed familiar."

"That's because the playwright is an unknown by the name of Harrison Rhodes. The theater allows me to use my own work for the acting classes, and I'm keeping my fingers crossed that one day they'll produce one of my plays."

"Maybe I'll be good enough to audition by then," Candy said, with a smile.

"Just think, you could give yourself and the playwright a five-star review."

"Consider it done!" she said, happy to further the conversation.

"Candy, I heard you turn down Matthew's offer for a cup of coffee, but the Mocha Café makes a mean latte. How about it? We don't have to stay late, and I'll even tell you who murdered the butcher. After all, you do owe me something for giving you and Matthew a mystery to rehearse," Hal said. "You two were supposed to have a love scene, but something made me change my mind at the last minute. How about it?"

It was almost worth hearing the inevitable "I told you so" from her mother as Candy said, "Now that's an offer I can't refuse."

THE BIG HEIST

"Hey Stan," Al shouted out from the kitchen. "That's the truck. Another load's here and it's about time. How 'bout giving me a hand?"

It was Friday at Kip's Lobster Shack, the day that Seaside Purveyors delivered fancy shellfish for the weekend. Al, the head chef, was responsible for receiving the supplies. Stan, the restaurant's bookkeeper, was always glad to take a break from paying bills to help out his co-worker. The two men had worked together for several years and had a pleasant easy-going friendship.

"Freddy's late again," Al said to Stan, who joined him in the kitchen.

"When isn't he late? We better bring him some strong

coffee because knowing Freddy, he's probably snoozing away. I don't know how he keeps that job with all the driving he has to do," Stan said, clucking like a concerned mother hen. "It's a miracle he doesn't fall asleep at the wheel."

The two men exited through the kitchen's back door to unload the crates of lobster, shrimp, and crabs. Friday's shipment was always a big one and today's was no exception. Kip's would be crowded over the weekend with hopefuls waiting at the bar for a free table, in addition to the seasoned regulars who knew enough to make reservations. As predicted, Freddy had already dozed off while waiting the few minutes for them.

"Wake up, old man! Let's get going," said Al, in a familiar way. "Stan has to get back to the books, and delivery should've been here an hour ago. You're holding up the works."

"Oh, you guys ready for me? I was just resting my eyes for a second," Freddy said, slurring his words.

Al and Stan gave each other a knowing look. Freddy had been drinking on the job again. He'd been with Seaside as a driver for fifteen years and, by some miracle, had never once been stopped for driving while intoxicated.

"Here you go, pal, a nice hot cup of coffee. That'll help straighten you out. Better drink it while Stan and I unpack our order. And take it easy on that hooch! I thought you were going to go to the AA meetings down by the church," Al said. "Wouldn't want anything to happen to our favorite driver."

"Yeah, I'll get around to it sooner or later. Don't worry about me. I know how to travel those back roads, nice and slow, and never seen a cop there yet. And boys, thanks for helping. My sciatica's acting up today, and it's worse if I have to get in and out of the truck," Freddy said, and sipped his coffee so he wouldn't have to explain further.

"There's always an excuse why Freddy wants to stay in the truck," Al whispered to Stan.

"Yeah, he's tipsy; that's for sure," Stan said. "Hopefully, the coffee will sober him up before his next delivery."

Later that day Al asked Stan to join him in the kitchen. Al had two mugs of coffee ready, and half of a day-old, but still fresh, pecan pie.

"Thought you could use a break about now," said Al. "Come on, have a seat and wait till you try this pie."

"You're right. Those numbers are beginning to spin around in my head, and whoa, that pie looks awesome," said Stan, raising his eyebrows in anticipation.

"Yep, left over from last night. We had a private party, friends of Kip's, and they ordered a bunch of desserts. All gone except this," he said, taking a bite. "Hmm, tastes as good as it looks."

"Where you getting the baked goods from these days?" Stan said, while piercing the pie with his fork. "You're right. It's delicious."

"New place in town. They call it Marie Antoinette's. Cute name. I told Kip when he hired me that I wasn't much of a baker and asked him to outsource his desserts. He agreed and now even lets me have the final say on which supplier to use. I can tell you that these folks are top notch," Al said. "Most of our customers probably don't realize that the desserts aren't made here, but we have the restaurant's reputation to think of, so it's got to be first-rate goods."

"They sure know how to make a pecan pie," Stan said, cutting himself another slice. "Got any whipped cream hiding in the fridge?"

The two men sat together chatting for a short time while devouring the pie smothered in cream. Then Al spoke up.

"Buddy, I'm going to get right down to business. I've figured out an easy way for us to make some quick cash, and I wanna discuss it before my staff comes back. We have about fifteen minutes."

Stan put his fork down. He wanted to give his full attention to Al. With his daughter, Juliette, going off to college in the fall Stan had been nervous about coming up with enough money for all the extras he and his wife wanted to provide for her. They spoiled their only child and had no plans to let Juliette arrive at school without a new wardrobe packed in the finest luggage. Even with his other part-time job at a small real estate firm in town and his wife's teaching salary, they were still falling short of the expenses coming their way.

"Fire away," said Stan, anxious, but not wanting to appear too eager. Al had come up with some doozies in the past, and fortunately had never followed through with any of his get-rich-quick schemes.

"You know I do all the food ordering for Kip's, and you take care of the bills. Just think how simple it would be for me to order in extra shellfish for Friday's deliveries—enough to supply the restaurant for the weekend—and enough to supply us with a trunk full of lobster, because that's the most popular with folks, to sell up at the pier on the weekends. We'll make a fortune. I'll keep those crawlers alive on ice in my extra coolers till I'm ready to go home. Early Saturday morning we can drive up to Rockport and sell the goods to some of the smaller shops and any tourists hanging around. We can hawk those beauties on the cheap, and since Seaside doesn't service that area, it'll never get back to Kip.

I'll have plenty of time to get back here for the dinner crowd and you can go on home or to your other job. My kitchen helpers don't get here till about two and they're not the sharpest tacks in the tool box. No way they're going to catch on. We don't serve lunch on Saturdays, so it should all go like clockwork. All you have to do is pay Seaside's invoices like you always do."

Stan was silent for a moment before speaking up.

"That's illegal, Al. It's called stealing. Kip has been pretty good to us over the years, and he trusts us. He lets you have the final say on what bakery to use, and he's never once questioned anything in my department. This isn't a great way to pay him back."

"Kip makes more money than he knows what to do with, and you're right, he never looks at the provisions list or the checkbook. With his prices, he won't lose money even if we over order once in a while. I'm not saying we should do it every weekend, but even if we did Memorial Day to start, we'd clean up, and that's just around the corner. After that, the season kind of dries up for lobster, but we could jump in again right after Labor Day when the tourists are still running wild and the shops can hardly keep up with the demand. That'd give us a good spread."

"True enough, and if we do one, maybe two, Saturdays a month Kip probably won't take notice," Stan said, going against his better judgment and his conscience.

"Kip only comes in right before the dinner crowd to meet and greet. And didn't he ask you to do his kid's algebra homework all last year? I bet he never paid you extra," Al said.

Al was right. Stan had put in a lot of extra hours doing that whiney kid's homework as well as coming up with a household budget for Kip's beautiful, but flaky wife, Alice. He'd never asked for overtime and Kip never offered it. Stan kept the books, paid bills, and was never off as much as a penny. He was well paid and thankful that he had the job, but still...

"What about Freddy?" Stan said. "Won't he notice that we're taking more off the truck than usual even if he's not involved in packing it? And what if he decides to help us unload? That'd be just our luck."

"Good point, Stan, but I've already thought of that. In case he wants to help out, which is almost one hundred percent doubtful, we'll have his coffee all ready for him, only this time it'll be topped off with whiskey to make sure he stays put. He can have his forty winks, plus."

"Hold up there! We can't do that. It's way too dangerous," Stan said. "That's the worst plan ever. I don't want us to be responsible for getting Freddy drunk, and possibly crashing the truck and hurting himself or anyone else. Come on, Al. Forget about this crazy idea."

"Not just yet, because I've already thought of everything you said and I agree with you; so here's what we're gonna do. I'll call Seaside and tell them to make us their last stop, so Freddy won't have any other deliveries. They won't care; I'll invent some reason. After his coffee, we'll insist that he take a nap in the back room on that old Army cot. We'll tell him he looks too tired to drive and that we'd prefer him to 'rest his eyes' before he gets back on the road."

"Let me do a little figuring," Stan said. "I'm not thrilled with working this scam, but like you said, maybe if we keep it small we'd get away with it. I spent a lot of hours doing that lazy kid's homework, and Alice couldn't follow a budget to save her life, so I'm going to consider this my bonus."

The two men discussed the details of the heist and decided to put their scheme into action the following Friday. Al was sure everything would go like clockwork, they'd have a nice side business collecting cash under the table, and no one would be the wiser.

On Monday morning, Al dialed Seaside to order extra provisions for a few imaginary upcoming parties.

"Seaside Purveyors, how may I help you?" said Wendy, who was the business's order taker, receptionist, secretary, and office manager all rolled into one. Wendy practically ran the place.

"Hey, girl! How's my favorite sweetie of the sea?" Al said.

"Just fine, Julius Child!" she answered, immediately recognizing his voice.

"Got a favor to ask of you. I have a bigger than usual order for the weekend so when Freddy brings the stuff around on Friday, can you make it his last stop? That way I'll have extra time to clear out the fridge to make room for everything, and he won't keep another appointment waiting," Al said. "Does that work out okay with your schedule?"

"For you, anything. Wish I had a hundred more customers like you. You get your orders in early, and pay on time. When ya gonna take me out to dinner?" Wendy said.

"Whenever your six-foot-three husband lets me," Al said, continuing to kid around with her. "You know I love you, but you're taken."

They went on with their convivial patter a few more minutes, and then Al placed the order.

"I'll take the regular, but better double up on the lobsters," he said.

"Wow, that's a huge order. Kip must be doing some business over there," she said.

"Yeah, things are rolling right along. A lot of big parties lately, plus our regulars. No complaints. Thanks doll, and we appreciate your superb service," Al said.

"Our pleasure, honey. Take care, and say hi to Stan, the money man," Wendy said.

On Friday after the lunch crowd left, and while the staff was still on break, Al was preparing some greens for the restaurant's popular chopped salad when he heard Seaside's truck pull up around three o'clock. He called for Stan to give him a hand with the deliveries as usual, and poured a mug of piping hot coffee for Freddy, only this time it was sweetened with a couple of ounces of Irish whiskey. He didn't think he'd get any complaints from the driver.

"Stan, let's go. The truck's here. I've got the extra coolers ready to go. After we get Freddy inside and all comfy on the cot, I'll load them up while you take in the regular order. Smooth as silk, and my staff won't be back here for another half hour. I told them to take a little more time today because tonight's first reservation isn't till seven."

Al and Stan went out though the kitchen door and walked toward the front of the truck to greet Freddy.

"Hey, Freddy, you in there? How's it going," Al said. "Hope we didn't wake you."

"Yeah, come on out. Got a nice cuppa joe waiting for you," Stan said, opening the door of the truck's cab.

"Hello, guys, you must be Al and Stan," said the man at the wheel. "My name's Chase Baldwin, and I'm Seaside's new driver."

Chase, a fit man about fifty, hopped out of the front seat and shook hands with the men.

"What happened to Freddy?" said Al, with a startled look. "Is he okay?"

"Oh, they had to retire poor old Freddy from delivery duty. Seems he got stopped by a police officer on his way back to Seaside a couple of days ago for drunk driving. Hit a few bushes. Good thing he was going slow so didn't do much damage to the truck. The boss put his foot down and is making sure that Freddy attends the AA meetings. They're giving him some desk work in the office and the warehouse, you know, helping out with inventory. I'm not sure they'll put him back as a driver because he's getting a little shaky for that, and some of the customers complain that he never gets out of the truck to unload like he's supposed to," Chase said.

Al stole a look at Stan, who stood there dumbstruck.

"Yeah, right. We stopped asking him to help a long time ago. He stays in the cab while we unload," Al said, trying to keep his voice steady. "Didn't realize it was a problem for other customers."

"He's not in jail, is he?" Stan asked, coming out of his zombie-like stance.

"He had to go to court, and the judge took his license away for a year and hit him up with a stiff fine. Threw him in the slammer until Wendy bailed him out. She's keeping tabs on him. Good thing Freddy never took the highway, so it's a blessing nobody was hurt."

"Freddy always takes the back roads. How'd they catch him?" Al said.

"Just so happened that a traffic cop followed him from one of his other delivery stops because he noticed that the truck was doing a bit of weaving," Chase said.

"So, you'll be working for Seaside now?" Al said.

"You got it. The whole thing turned out pretty good for me because I used to be on the same force with the arresting officer, and he called to let me know that Seaside would probably be looking for a new driver," Chase said.

Al tried to compose himself, while Stan stood there sweating profusely.

"I retired from the force a couple of years ago, but my wife said I was too young to sit around the house and do nothing, so I'm taking over Freddy's route," Chase said. "Hey, what's that you're holding? I hope it's coffee because I could sure use a cup. I'm getting that mid-afternoon slump."

"It's coffee alright," Al said, trying to cover up his angst, and poured the whiskey-reinforced beverage onto the ground, "but it's been sitting around too long. Come on into the kitchen with us and I'll make a fresh pot. Do you have time?"

"Sure do. Hey, that's real nice of you. Wendy scheduled Kip's for the last stop of the day, so I can get my coffee on here instead of hanging out at the diner. Give the wife a little more 'me' time, as she calls it. Then I'll help you unload. The stuff stays cold in the truck," Chase said.

"Thanks," Al said. "I guess you're right about Freddy getting too old to be a driver."

"I'm just glad he didn't hurt himself or anyone else," Stan added.

"The boss was pretty tough on him. Told him he had to go to AA from now on or he'd be out any kind of a job at Seaside. Wendy and I agreed to take turns driving him down to the church for meetings," Chase said.

"Yeah, that's what we've been telling him, but we shoulda made sure it was happening," Stan said. "Come on inside."

"In a minute. Wendy wanted me to check something with you. The boss has got Freddy helping out in the office, and he happened to notice your order for today. He mentioned that it seemed way too large, and there must be some mistake. Wendy told him that Al specifically ordered twice the usual amount of lobsters, but Freddy insisted that she double check it. Guess she didn't have time to call you, so they decided to pack the regular amount. She said I should ask you about it when I got here.

Wendy told me you were good guys, never any funny business, so there was no need to ask Kip about the order. Hate to inconvenience you, but if you still need those extra lobsters I'll be happy to go pick them up. Won't take more than twenty minutes there and back. I'm new on the job and I didn't want to go over anyone's head. The coffee can wait. I'll call the office now and tell her to get them ready," Chase said, slowly taking out his cell phone.

"Uh, you know what, you don't have to do that. I think Al here was overestimating the weekend crowd when he placed the order. We were hoping to have some large parties booked for the weekend, but turned out they canceled. Our regular order will do us just fine," Stan said, giving Al a knowing glance that meant, "It's over, pal."

"I hate to admit it, Chase, but Stan's right. I kinda screwed up on that. Glad you guys caught it. I guess Freddy's a whole lot sharper when he's not drinking. Why don't the three of us bring in the order, and I'll stick it in the fridge. Then, I'll put the coffee on," Al said.

"Got any pie to go with it?" Stan asked, with a relieved look on his face.

"Yep, leftover banana cream," Al said.

"You guys are the best," Chase said. "That's my favorite. And, I'll take care of everything back in the office. After all it was an honest mistake."

"Thanks, Chase. Let's party up and then it's business as usual," Al said, as he imagined hundred dollar bills with wings flying out of reach.

CATERING
TO LOVE

At the Walkers' annual Christmas party, which happens to be my third assignment for Rita's Down Home Caterers, I spot a situation that might threaten my relationship with a co-worker. The Walkers told me to pull out all the stops for their party and not to be concerned about the cost. Dream clients for any business, plus they were wonderfully easy to work with.

The evening's going along as planned until I notice that Mick, the head chef, is smuggling out a standing rib roast, a dozen baby lamb chops with a container of Rita's special recipe mint jelly, and a tray of miniature pastries. The problem is that if I report Mick to my boss, Rita, he'll probably get fired; but if I keep quiet about it, the client will be paying for food that is either supposed to be served at the party or returned to our catering kitchen. I hesitate to speak up because some chefs can be very touchy and Mick is no exception, but my first responsibility is to Rita.

"Mick, where are you going with that stuff," I ask, making sure I'm out of range from the servers that have been hired for the festivities.

"To another gig. We're swamped this time of year. You think I only handle one party a weekend in December? No way. Don't worry about it, newbie. Everything's under control. I'll be back later to help with the clean up. The waiters know the ropes; can't understand why it's such a surprise to you," he says in an annoyed tone. Mick takes off and yells back at me, fracturing my name in the process, "If you have any questions, text me. See ya around, Mathilde."

I only know of two additional parties Rita has booked that night, but Maria and Dave, our other chefs, are covering those. Since I'm the new kid on the block I might have missed something, but Mick's hurried departure doesn't look good.

I had decided to represent Rita's company, a successful family business, after working for several years as the assistant food and beverage manager for a large chain hotel. It was grueling work with a demanding boss, and absolutely no creativity allowed in the food preparation. As a party planner for Rita's I could devise appealing and up-to-date menus for the clients, and supervise the events to make sure everything would go accordingly. When I mentioned the switch to my best friend, Kristin, she hadn't been so sure about it.

"Not a good idea," Kristin said, "they'll have you working nights and weekends, and you'll never meet anyone. It won't be like your nine-to-five at the hotel."

"No problem. I'm happy to be out of there, plus I'm not ready to meet anyone yet. I've got to get on track with my career, and I think working for a smaller company will do it...you know, be a big fish in a small pond? I can bring corporate ideas to Rita's, only scaled down," I said. Knowing that Kristin was about to bring up Shane, my ex-husband, I decided to connect the dots for her. "You might not get this, but I actually want to fill my nights and weekends. It's lonely without him and for now, working parties will have to do."

"I do get it, but it's time you started dating again," Kristin said, "It's been almost a year since you and Shane broke up. And just because your ex acted like a frat boy doesn't mean every other man is going to behave like he did. You haven't even given yourself a chance yet."

"It wasn't only his fault," I said, not wanting to start any ex-bashing. "A lot of it was on me. You know how pushy I can be. A man's entitled to be with his friends, whether I like them or not. I was pretty hard on him about that. I guess we grew apart because we didn't have nearly enough in common to begin with. Opposites attract? Maybe, but it didn't stick."

"Mathilde, I'm going to give it to you straight. I know you better than anyone, and honey, we all slip up in relationships. You think it's all milk and honey with Keith and me? No way! We have plenty of battles, but the foundation is sound, and I don't think you and Shane had that. It's time to accept the fact that the two of you should have remained friends, and not gotten married. You'll find a guy who's as perfect for you as you say your job is, but you have to get out there and meet them, and that's not going to happen if you're working nights and weekends," she said, driving home her point.

"You done?" I said. "Because if that lecture goes on any longer, I'll need a nap."

"Come on," she said, looking at her watch. "I'll give you another few minutes to feel sorry for yourself, but see if you can walk and talk at the same time. I need ice cream and you need a decent haircut."

Kristin was probably right about my not wanting to socialize, but in the meanwhile I wouldn't have to be alone during the times I was used to sharing with my ex-husband. I'd be with a congenial crew who made me feel like part of their family. Of course, it wasn't the same as going out to dinner and a movie with a partner, but, unfortunately, after a year and a half of marriage it became clear that Shane hadn't been interested in spending that much time together. Several nights a week he'd go out with the guys, grab a few beers and a hot dog, and come home long after I'd fallen asleep. It was a constant tug of war, and we were rarely on the same side.

The dream I'd had of preparing fun dinners together with my husband never came to pass. When I suggested counseling sessions, he agreed, but a few months later it was obvious that we couldn't make a go of it. It was a sad time for Shane and me and about the only idea that we agreed on was a separation, and eventually a divorce, if either of us wanted to find happiness in the future. Shane and I managed to remain friends, but without children to bind us together, it was more of a cordial quick hello when we bumped into each other.

I enjoyed my initial consultations with the hosts of each party I planned—getting to know their likes and dislikes in regard to food, tableware, and the type of wine they preferred, although some opted instead for a variety of soft drinks.

The Walkers were particularly outgoing and pleasant to work with. During our first appointment, they'd set out a silver coffee service and some mouth-watering pecan rolls while we went over the details of the Christmas party. They gave me a tour of their lovely home and showed me photos of their children and grandchildren. I admired the Christmas tree decorated to the hilt, which stood in the corner of their oversized living room, and I mentioned the tasteful Nativity scene that graced their front lawn. By the end of the hour, I felt like I'd known the Walkers for years. I was determined to give them a spectacular party.

My first two jobs for Rita's had gone smoothly. A church luncheon with all the trimmings, and a bridal shower had been successful. I'd handed out business cards to prospective clients at both functions, and Rita was pleased with my work. I always met with her and the appointed chef to go over my menus in case they had any suggestions or problems with the selections. I was anxious to learn, and Rita believed in me. Mick had been especially pleased with the Walkers' Christmas menu and I assumed, after watching him walk away with hundreds of dollars worth of food, that it was because he could make a healthy profit reselling the expensive provisions or stocking his own freezer.

I excused myself from the Walkers' buffet table to address my first big problem—an apparent theft. I call Rita on my cell phone.

"Hi Mathilde, how's it going?" my boss says, answering on the first ring.

"Fine, but I need to check something out with you. Is there another party on for tonight where Mick's doing the cooking?"

Silence at the other end of the phone.

"Hello?"

"Did he disappear with some food giving you that story?" asks Rita.

I hesitate before verifying what she appears to already know.

"This is the second time he's done that," Rita continues, "I gave him another chance a few months ago, but I can't afford to do that again. I'll have to fire him. Do you think you can handle the rest of the evening on your own if he doesn't come back in time?"

"I'm sure I can. We're almost up to dessert, and the coffee is ready to go," I calmly reassure her. Myself? Not so much. Without Mick there to help oversee the servers and the bartender, who knows what'll happen?

"Okay then, see you in the office at the next meeting. Oh, and, Mathilde, thanks."

The staff at Rita's meets every Monday to discuss the previous week's parties and upcoming events. Today Rita announces that she has fired Mick for stealing.

"We can't charge the client for things we're not supplying. That means food and service. If you're supposed to set up for a party at five o'clock and you get there an hour late, we're cheating the customer. That's as bad as stealing food. Sooner or later dishonesty will ruin our reputation and I'll be out of business. I'm sure none of you wants to be out of work," Rita says, as serious as she's ever been. There's no joking around today.

"Gee, Rita, I certainly don't," Dave says. "Laine has a high-risk pregnancy and she's on complete bed rest for the next two months. I had a feeling something was up with that guy. How'd you find out?"

"Mathilde called me to report the theft. Mick will find another job, and hopefully he's learned his lesson. Believe it or not, he actually tried to filch a couple of pans of *Chicken Piccata* from a condo party a while back. The client called me and I covered for him saying there must have been something wrong with the entrée, and the chef probably pulled it. I spoke to Mick about it and he coughed up some excuse, so I gave him the benefit of the doubt and let him stay on. He's a top-notch chef, one of the best I've ever had work here, but I can't put up with that type of conduct. And Dave, take home some salmon for Laine's dinner," Rita says.

I'm aware of everyone's gaze toward me when Rita reveals her source. I feel like a stool pigeon until I notice that there is one unfamiliar face smiling at me. It belongs to a tall blond man with the kind of bluish-green eyes and high cheekbones I'd kill for.

"Most of you know Casey, he used to chef for us," Rita says, motioning to the smiling man. "Casey's been working in France for the past year and has brought back some sensational recipes. When he called to see if there were any openings, I invited him to come to our meeting this morning and I hired him. Mathilde, since Mick's gone, you and Casey will be in charge of the Logan wedding scheduled for June. You both have the most experience with large parties, and I'm sure you'll work well together. You might want to catch each other up before your presentation to the client on Friday. The Logans want everything in place well before June."

Rita calls the meeting to an end, and I go back to my desk to start planning a menu for the Logans. I don't care how beautiful Casey's aquamarines are, he just better like my suggestions. I'm not thrilled about having to deal with another temperamental chef, but at least Casey is trustworthy or Rita never would have rehired him. Now that Casey knows I ratted out Mick he might be wary of me, but the smile he threw my way this morning makes me think otherwise. While I'm working at my computer, Dave stops by my desk.

"You did the right thing, Mathilde. Mick's been stealing

from Rita for months, mostly bits and pieces, small stuff, but still, none of us had the guts to say anything to her because he's been the head chef around here forever. I can't believe he had the nerve to take a whole roast plus the trimmings this time. No one holds it against you," Dave says, consoling me. "Why don't you come to Casey's place tonight? He posted a notice in the kitchen with his address inviting everyone. He's probably going to prepare some of his French specialties for the gang as his own welcome back party. Laine's insisting that I don't have to stay home and babysit her, so I'd be glad to pick you up after I make her dinner…around seven? How about it?"

Just what I need. Our new chef showing off with a gourmet party featuring fattening foods and rich French desserts. After being Miss Goody Two-Shoes, or Benedict Arnold, depending on how you look at it, I certainly don't want to follow it up with being a party pooper. I'm also somewhat intrigued by Casey, so I agree to go. Maybe I'll bring along some fancy appetizers to show Casey I'm a team player. I almost text Kristin to tell her about the party, but I don't have time to play twenty questions.

I get home in time to pull out a few cookbooks before settling on a complicated, but familiar, recipe involving puff pastry filled with spinach, mushrooms and Feta cheese. I make a few dozen, wrap them up, change into what I think looks like a Parisian outfit, and wait for Dave to pick me up. I make a note to thank Kristin for taking me to her stylist because, for once, my hair is behaving.

We arrive at Casey's, and after saying hello to everyone I slip into the kitchen to heat up my appetizers. Casey is nowhere to be seen, and neither are all the saucepans I imagined would be simmering on the stove by now.

"Huh! Where's all that gourmet French stuff?" I say aloud to what appears to be an empty kitchen. "Some party."

"I thought you guys would prefer a little simple food for a change," I hear a voice behind me say. "That's why I ordered in chicken wings, ribs and coleslaw," says Casey, his Caribbean blue green eyes crinkling up as he smiles. "I did bake the cornbread, but I'm not sure if that counts as gourmet food."

"I'm really sorry, Casey. I hope I didn't offend you," I say, trying to hide my embarrassment.

"Sorry? About what?" he says, pretending he didn't hear my outburst.

When he starts to laugh, I do too.

"So, whatcha got there?" he says, peeking under one of the foil wrapped trays I'd place on the counter.

"Some starters I thought you'd like to try. But I don't know if they'll go with the rest of your menu," I say.

"I have a better idea, Mathilde," Casey says, pronouncing my name with just the right accent. "Why don't you put them in the fridge and tomorrow night I'll cook a real French dinner for the two of us. You already have the French name! How about it?"

I begin to feel a little warm, even though the oven is off, when I tell Casey he has a date.

Just as I'm thinking about how much fun it would be to cook with Casey, he takes my hand and says, "Something tells me we're going to be spending a lot of time in the kitchen together."

Something tells me he's right.

POETRY IN MOTION

Carrie Thomas looked up from her counter as soon as she heard the bell jingle at the entry door. *Second Chance*, the consignment store where she had a part-time job, accepted merchandise for resale every Wednesday after three o'clock.

"Good afternoon, Mr. Snyder," she said, with a pasted-on smile hoping to disguise the annoyance in her voice. Carrie had been in the middle of composing what she hoped would be a prize-winning poem when Mr. Snyder entered the spacious shop with a load of books and a stack of linens. The last thing she needed was an interruption, and Mr. Snyder was long-winded. She'd have to find some excuse to cut short his time with her.

On the other hand, his items were usually salable, not that it made a difference in Carrie's paycheck. She'd wanted to work on commission because of her amazing knack for displaying items and following through with a sale, but Mr. Dobbs, her boss and the owner, decided to stick with a set salary for her. "Don't want that much bookkeeping," he'd told her after his wife, Margaret, passed away. Margaret had been the brains of the business, and saw in Carrie a determined young lady ready to work hard to help continue the growth and profitability of *Second Chance*, notwithstanding her uneven disposition. The two women had been in the process of basing part of Carrie's salary on commission when Margaret took ill and a week later, she was gone. Carrie almost left *Second Chance*, not caring to deal with Mr. Dobbs, but she knew it would look unsympathetic to their customers in the tight-knit town of Devon, New Hampshire, where she lived, worked, and went to school. Plus, Carrie had bigger plans for those customers and needed them on her good side.

"Hi there, Carrie, looking pretty as always. Nice hair style too. What'd they call that?" he said.

"Thanks. It's a French braid. So, how can I help you?" she said, trying to move the conversation along.

"Whatcha doing there? Writing one of your poems? I heard you made it into the big competition over at Hampshire College. You sure are a busy gal going to school, working, and writing poetry. You gotta do it while you're young," Mr. Snyder said, oblivious to Carrie's impatience. Like Mr. Dobbs, he was an elderly widower lonely for female companionship, not that Carrie, who was young enough to be his granddaughter, was in the running. Mr. Snyder had previously told her that his sights were set on the lovely Miss Peppercorn, who worked at the library and who always seemed to have time for a pleasant conversation with him.

"As a matter of fact, that's exactly what I was doing. I was lucky to be accepted into the competition," she said. "I submitted my application on the first day, and only thirty of us got in."

Hampshire College was a branch of the state university that Carrie planned to attend after completing her associate's degree at Beacon, the two-year community college that was on Hampshire's campus. Her parents had been victims of a Ponzi-type scheme, and if it weren't for the scholarship she'd won after being named valedictorian of her high school senior class, Carrie wouldn't even have been able to attend Beacon. There was no way her parents could have covered the tuition at Hampshire if Carrie had begun there as a freshman. The way things were with their financial situation, they barely had enough to scrape together to pay for their daughter's extra costs at Beacon.

"Carrie, I know you want to apply to Hampshire after you graduate Beacon and we'll do the best we can," her dad told her. "We're going to sell the house and take an apartment in a less expensive community until I can build up our savings again. I've been offered a steady position as the foreman of a construction company over in Bedford, and Mom's already been hired to manage a day care center, so we'll help all we can. Your car's running pretty well, and it's not a bad commute."

"Dad, all my friends are in Devon and I already have a part-time job at *Second Chance,*" she said. "Please let me stay here; I don't want to move to another town and have to drive the highway to school. Maybe by the time I finish at Beacon, things will be better for you and Mom, and if I can get some kind of funding for Hampshire, it might work out. I'm saving most of my salary so please think about it. The hours a week I'll have to spend commuting will take away from my studies and I'm already stretched."

"Your mom and I are so proud of you. Too bad we were real suckers. A good life lesson, but unfortunately we lost most of our savings. The upside is that Mom and I are both young and strong enough to rebuild our lives and as soon as things straighten out for us, we'll help you transfer with or without a scholarship. Your mother put the house on the market last week, and the real estate agent already has a decent offer," Mr. Thomas said. "Honey, I know you don't want to move, but I don't see how we can let you stay here by yourself."

"Dad, I'm almost nineteen so don't worry about me. Focus on getting things settled for you guys. What if I found a safe place to stay here in Devon? You know my friend Samantha from Buffalo, right? She told me that Beacon provides housing for out-of-state students, and maybe under the circumstances they'll give me a spot in one of the dorms. She's really happy living there. I mean the rooms are small, but she doesn't have to worry about cooking or getting snowed in. She's on the food plan, and if you and Mom can't handle that part, I can pitch in with my salary," Carrie said. "What do you think about that idea?"

Mr. Thomas knew that his strong-willed daughter would win in the end, so decided to accept a compromise that would be affordable in a secure setting.

"I have to admit that would be an ideal solution. I think Mom would agree if I can swing it financially. That way you could still keep your day job, go to school, and we'll try to visit on the weekends. I'll call Beacon and see if I can make arrangements. Best to be up front with them."

Once Mr. Thomas explained the family's unfortunate circumstances, Beacon agreed to give Carrie a room at a discounted rate for the rest of the time she'd be in attendance.

Her scholarship would remain in full force provided she kept her grades up, which the dean knew wouldn't be a problem. Carrie was one of Beacon's most promising students.

Hampshire College was going to present the first annual National Poetry Month Competition, sponsored by ten local businesses. The prize was five thousand dollars, an almost unheard of amount for a poetry contest, and a big enough purse to create an enormous amount of interest in poetry at the college, and in the community at large.

Carrie had competed in local poetry contests held in neighboring bookstores and coffee shops where she'd won several times, but the prizes were usually a free cappuccino in the cafés, or a ten-dollar gift certificate. If she could capture the big prize, she'd have almost enough, along with her other savings, to realize her dream and pay a few months' rent on another consignment shop across town. It was a run-down place that didn't do nearly the amount of business that Mr. Dobbs's store did. Carrie's goal was to eventually buy the store from the owner, Mrs. Frane, an elderly woman who wanted to sell her house, her business, and retire to Florida.

If Carrie could earn a full scholarship to Hampshire, she'd attend classes at night and attend to the business during the day. Eventually, she'd have to hire an assistant after she fixed up Mrs. Frane's place to get it running smoothly.

I'll be crazy busy, but it'll all be worth it. I'll have my associate degree from Beacon, then finish up at Hampshire, and have a ready-made business in my pocket.

"How about taking a look at some of these other things I brought in."

"Sure, Mr. Snyder," Carrie said, jolted out of her lengthy daydream while he perused the shop's merchandise. She hoped to get him out of the store as quickly as possible, but had to be polite and friendly if she wanted to retain him as a future client. Mrs. Frane's consignment store had a small clientele that Carrie would expand by adding Mr. Dobbs's customers. She was sure she could lure them away from *Second Chance* and double the salary she was making now. Mr. Dobbs had no idea about running a successful business. His two sons had no interest in their father's shop, and it was only a matter of time before Mr. Dobbs would be out of business without Carrie in charge.

"Let's see, we can take these dishes and tablecloths; those patterns are very popular and should sell right away," Carrie said, placing them on a wrought iron rack.

"What about these old books? There's a few on gardening, and even one on poetry. Found them in the back of the bookcase. They were my late wife's, bless her soul. Give me a good thriller anytime, but I thought you could put these on the sale table in the side room," Mr. Snyder said.

Carrie started to say that *Second Chance* didn't usually deal in books until she glanced at one of the titles, *Wings of Poetry* by Professor Lawrence Rose. Carrie had never heard of him, and when she looked at the inside cover she saw that the leather bound book was a first edition, published in 1970.

"Sure, Mr. Snyder, this might sell. I'll put the right price on it."

"Thanks, Carrie, you know this book is out of print, so maybe it's more valuable than we think," he said.

"I'll check it out on Amazon and eBay, and if it's not there, I can put a higher price tag on it. I'll give you a call when we sell your things."

They chatted for a few more minutes until she was able to usher him out.

"Bye, Mr. Snyder, come back and visit again soon."

"Sure thing, Carrie. And good luck at that big contest. I think I'll stop by to cheer you on," he said. "Right now I'm going to head over to the library to invite Miss Peppercorn to join me there."

As soon as Mr. Snyder left, she opened Professor Rose's book. Carrie began to read some of the poems and found they were extremely visual and unusually appealing. The poem she had been working on seemed amateurish compared to those of Lawrence Rose's. If only she could write like he did, she'd be sure to win the big competition. A light bulb lit above her head and she realized how she could manage to hook the big prize. She would take a phrase or line here and there from each of the sixty-eight poems in Lawrence Rose's book, and piece them all together in a contemporary new-age poem that would read beautifully, even mysteriously, and the interpretation would be left up to the listener's imagination. Carrie came up with a perfect title: *Collage*.

What she was doing would be considered plagiarism, and if anyone found out she would be disqualified and humiliated in the community, and possibly sued or fined. She'd never get into Hampshire, and would probably be kicked out of Beacon. But how many people had ever heard of the obscure poet, Lawrence Rose? Even if they did, it was unlikely that anyone would be able to link her *Collage* to the lines she'd extract from his poems. Hadn't Mr. Snyder said that the book was out of print? She did another search on the Internet and couldn't find mention of *Wings of Poetry*. The only article on Lawrence Rose was that he'd gone into seclusion in Newfoundland decades ago, and no one had heard from him since.

Carrie threw away the draft she was working on when Mr. Snyder had interrupted her, and put together a new poem with a little help from Professor Rose's *Wings of Poetry*. She was sure it would be the winning entry. Carrie made a note to tell Mr. Snyder that she decided to buy the book for herself…she couldn't risk anyone else reading those poems.

The following week Carrie visited the dilapidated two-story building that housed *Retro & More* in the large storefront space. She was meeting with Mrs. Mollie Frane, the owner of the consignment business she had her eye on.

"Hello, Carrie, come on in. There's some coffee and cookies in the back. Would you mind fixing us a snack?" Mrs. Frane said. "I feel kind of sluggish today. No fun getting older!"

"Sure thing, Mrs. Frane," Carrie said, gearing up to be at her most charming. "Be back in a flash."

When Carrie returned with two mugs of coffee and a few chocolate chip cookies, she set it all down on one of the consignment store's old wooden tables, and pulled up two of the matching chairs.

"Thank you, dear." Mrs. Frane sat down and sighed as if she carried the weight of the world on her shoulders. "I don't know why I can't sell this dinette set. A nice round table with four sturdy chairs at only a hundred dollars for the whole kit and caboodle. And real wood, mind you, not that junk they use today. Who wouldn't want to have this in their home, but people just pass it by like they don't even see it."

Mrs. Frane knew that Carrie presently worked at *Second Chance,* and had heard that she'd increased their business substantially. Mrs. Frane had promised to keep their conversations confidential, which she was happy to do, because there was no love lost between Mr. Dobbs and her. They were competitors, but that was not the source of her displeasure. Mrs. Frane thought Mr. Dobbs would want to keep company with her after his wife passed. Mrs. Frane had brought over casseroles and her special pickled peppers in the weeks following Mrs. Dobbs's funeral, but all she got was a stiff "thank you." Carrie knew he had no interest in Mrs. Frane, and had tried to let her down gently, but the older woman was hurt and disappointed. If she could steal Carrie away from his business, she'd be only too happy to do so.

"Mrs. Frane, I don't mean to tell you how to run things, but you might want to think about changing the sign in this area to read Breakfast Room. Dinette is kind of old-fashioned wording. What I think would look great is to lightly sand the table top and put a fresh coat of stain on it. I'd spruce up the chair seats with some new upholstery, and maybe display the set with a few pretty placemats, and four of those vintage cranberry-glass plates you have on the shelves. Or, I'd totally refinish the table and paint it a hip color. That look is very in right now, and I bet when it's all redone you'd get close to three or four hundred. Like you said, it's solid wood, but it's all in the merchandising," Carrie said.

"Hmm, I never thought of doing all that, but I can't be dragging furniture out back to work on it. I'm too old for that, and it'd cost a pretty penny to hire someone," Mrs. Frane said.

"Oh, I agree, handymen charge a lot these days, and that's why I'd do it myself. I've done tons of that kind of work for *Second Chance*. That's one of the reasons our business increased the way it did," Carrie said.

"So I've heard. If I didn't own this building I'd go bankrupt. It's my nest egg. I've had fun over the years talking with customers, but it still gets lonely since my husband ran out on me, and with Mr. Dobbs not inviting me to the upcoming spring dance and all, well it's thumbs down on him," she said, punctuating her remark with two arthritic thumbs pointing to the floor. "Why, he didn't even send me a Christmas card after I brought over a homemade fruitcake!"

Mrs. Frane had also gifted Carrie with one of her fruitcakes, which Carrie immediately brought over to the soup kitchen where they gave her an exasperated look because several other donors, including Mr. Dobbs, had done the same.

"I need to take advantage of my remaining years, not waste them away. What's left for me here? These northern winters are so depressing, and it's coming up on April and I can still feel a chill. There are days I put up the closed sign on the door, and hole up in my upstairs apartment with a bowl of hot soup. I guess that's not great for business," Mrs. Frane said.

"No ma'am, it surely isn't," Carrie said, making a mental note about renting out the second floor apartment while she still had to live on campus. "Mrs. Frane, you have plenty of good years left, but I have to agree with you about the cold weather being a problem. More coffee?"

"Yes, please. Dear, that's why I want to move to Florida as soon as I can get someone to run the shop and take it over one day. I hope it will be you. Being in Florida means I wouldn't have to worry about a building, what with our winters being so severe. Who knows when a big storm could blow the roof off this place? And that louse of a husband and I were never blessed with children, so I have no one here to look after me in my old age. Carrie, you've been so kind to me, so if you're interested, I'll forego a down payment and we'll put your rent toward the purchase price. Then one day this damn place will belong to you, excuse my French!

This old building really isn't worth much because it's not in the best part of town, and it needs some renovations, and don't forget, I'll be living with my sister in Florida, which will keep my expenses down. My niece and her family are down there also so I won't be alone, or lonely. I want to do something good for you by making an arrangement with my business and the building," Mrs. Frane said. She was beginning to sound teary and Carrie decided it was time to take advantage of the frail senior citizen.

"Oh, Mrs. Frane, that would be incredible, and so kind of you," Carrie said. Her eyes lit up as she continued the conversation. "Can I tell you a secret? My dream is to own this business, or one like it. I've been saving ever since high school because I knew what I wanted even back then. I'm working toward my associate degree in business administration at Beacon, and if I'm able to score a scholarship to Hampshire, I'll get my Bachelor's in economics."

"I know your folks had some financial trouble a while back— sorry about that. I heard that a salesman ran off with their money and with a bunch of others, too. Terrible shame they never caught the crooks, but I bet the F.B.I. is working on it," Mrs. Frane said. "They had that nice lady agent come round to speak to me and a few others from church."

"Yes, and they have some good leads, but the money is gone. My parents decided to sell their house and downsize. They're moving a few towns over where my dad's been hired at a construction company, so they'll do alright. We're tough New Englanders."

"Your folks are doing what they have to do to survive, but where does that leave you? You can't be living out of town and running a business."

"I'm going to stay in one of Beacon's dorms. My dad's arranged it because my folks didn't want me in an apartment, even with roommates, and I'll be happy to stay there. I've got enough on my plate without worrying about keeping up my own place. As it is I have to plan classes around my work schedule, so living in the dorm solves all my housing problems," Carrie said. "It's really an awesome campus, and I'll save time and gas money by not commuting. I'm lucky that my dad bought me a car before losing most of their savings, so I can still get around town."

"You're going to be a busy little bee, working and going to school. I know you'll do well. Give your parents my best. If they want to consign anything, I'll send Ned out with the truck to do the pick up," Mrs. Frane said. "No charge."

"Thanks, I'll be sure to tell my mom," Carrie said.

"How about you begin work here in a month? I'll stay on for a week or so, but you know your way around. Then you can take over and start paying your mortgage off. How about if we say fifteen thousand for the business, and another thirty for the building?" Mrs. Frane said.

Even though the building was in poor repair, it still had to be worth at least twice that, but Carrie wasn't going to argue with a bargain. Forty-five thousand dollars was certainly beyond her reach now, but she had close to four thousand in the bank, money she'd saved from all the years she worked throughout high school, and her first year at Beacon. The prize money, which she was counting on, would help pay the rent, which would actually be going toward the purchase price. After that, Carrie was sure *Retro & More* would be bringing in a good income. Carrie knew that many of Mrs. Frane's items were priced far too low in the current market for vintage furniture and tableware, and she'd have no problem upping the tags for a better profit. She'd continue to take most of her classes at night or in the early morning and sooner or later, she'd own *Retro & More*.

"Oh, Mrs. Frane, are you certain? I want to be fair," she said.

"Honey, of course I'm sure. I know the building would go for more than that, but you can't put a price tag on an honest girl who works as hard as you do. And you can fix up the shop any way you like. Now you haven't mentioned your plans to Mr. Dobbs, have you? I know he's put a lot of money into his place because he probably thinks you're staying on. If he'd paid a little more attention to me rather than Miss Peppercorn down at the library, we could have had a nice combined business. The old coot! She's much too young for him, plus and I hear Mr. Snyder is keeping company with her. She certainly gets around for a librarian!" Mrs. Frane said, with a snort. "But you do have to tell him about our arrangement sooner or later."

"That's no problem. He doesn't come in much these days, and I'm sure his sons will be happy to take over for me," Carrie said, crossing her fingers behind her back. "He can teach the boys the business and I can stay on for a couple of weeks to train them. They haven't shown much interest in working there and they might run the place into the ground, but at least it's a shot to own their own business one day," Carrie said.

"This town is big enough for more than one consignment shop. Just look over at Peach Place. They have bunches of stores over there."

"Yes, but those are charity thrift shops and they don't carry the same type of goods. They're all run by volunteers and the proceeds get donated to local places in need. You and Mr. Dobbs have two honest-to-goodness consignment shops, which makes him your only competition."

"Speaking of donations, if you see stuff sitting around here forever it's best to give it on over to the abused women's shelter run by the church down near Walnut Street and take a tax write-off. They'll even come pick it up, or you can ask Ned to drop it by on one of his runs. I was about to get rid of this dinette, or rather breakfast room set, but I think your idea is better," Mrs. Frane said.

"After I jazz it up, I'll send you a picture with a new price tag," Carrie said. "Mrs. Frane, how much money will I have to come up with to start out?"

"Let's say two months' rent, or I should say your first two-month mortgage payment and I'll also consider that as your down payment. I'll have my attorney write up all the papers and we can sign as soon as you think you'll have the money. When do you expect that might be?"

"I'll know in a couple of weeks. Can you hold out until then? You see, I'm entered into that big poetry contest over at Hampshire and I've been working every spare minute on a fantastic poem. If I win, I'll be five thousand dollars closer to my goal."

"I was planning on going to that event, so I'll be rooting for you. Five thousand, huh? Well, if you win, that'll cover the first four months. After that, I'll have to bump it up to fifteen hundred to be paid by the tenth of the month. Does that sound fair?" Mrs. Frane said.

"Yes, more than fair. Everyone's watching their budget in this down economy, so a good consignment shop is exactly what they need."

I know how much Mr. Dobbs pulls in monthly and I should be able to double or even triple that here, Carrie thought.

"You'll get to keep the accounts receivable after paying the bills. You'll have to take care of expenses, utilities, a little on advertising to let people know we exist, some petty cash items, and of course, money to Ned when he's on the job. I keep it all up here," she said, pointing to her head. "My memory is top notch, but I'll write it down because you'll probably want to use a computer program."

"Yes, Mrs. Frane, for sure I'll do that. I'm going to apply some of the business practices I'm learning in school and do your shop justice," Carrie said. "I won't disappoint you, and I appreciate your not asking for more of a down payment."

"I can manage with our arrangement as is. I know things are tight for you and your family. Don't forget, Carrie, I'm still a business woman. Been running this place for over forty years, so if you default on, let's say two months, I'll have to take back the shop, but I think you'll do fine," Mrs. Frane said, giving Carrie her signature thumbs up motion.

"Thanks for your confidence in me."

"Now, how about you go back in the kitchen and scare up a few more of these cookies?" Mrs. Frane said. "I really should make my fruitcake more than once a year; much better than the store-bought stuff!"

The day of the competition finally came. Carrie arrived at the college, and greeted a few of her classmates from Beacon, and friends from high school who were attending Hampshire.

"Hi, Carrie," said Eric Willis, "isn't this exciting? Five thousand dollars! Who'd a thought there'd ever be that much money in poetry. It would sure help pay part of my tuition next semester. How's it going at Beacon?"

"Couldn't be better. After I get my associate's, I hope to transfer here. Beacon has some fantastic business courses, but economics is where my head is at," Carrie said.

"You haven't changed a bit," said Eric, with a laugh. "Remember that lemonade stand your dad built way back when? You were the only kid making money and not drinking up the profits."

"Unfortunately, it wasn't enough to get into Hampshire. Maybe one day."

"Yeah, it'd be great to have you here. Sorry about that situation with your folks. So, what have you got going for today? I've written a traditional love sonnet, and I think it's my best work."

"Wait and see, Eric," she said. Carrie didn't want to give anyone a heads-up as to what she was going to read. "Let's just say it's not traditional."

The auditorium was filled with friends and families of the contestants, as well as college kids and the local business people who had contributed to the prize money. Carrie had asked her folks to attend, but they were still too embarrassed about the financial situation that had forced them to move away to face a crowd of former neighbors. All the poets were seated at long tables; their work in front of them. Carrie turned and waved to Mrs. Frane, who saluted her with two thumbs up.

Professor McArt began the contest by announcing the rules, and introducing the three professors from the English department who would be judging the competition. The thirty qualifying poets would read their finest work, one poem apiece, each entrant hoping to win the prize money. After hearing the first ten, and then fifteen more, Carrie knew the prize was in the bag. She had to admit that Eric's beautiful sonnet probably would have won were it not for her own poem, which was the next to the last entry. After Carrie read *Collage*, the staggering round of applause had practically assured her of coming in first. Mrs. Frane's thumbs were nearly going through the roof.

I've pulled it off and no one's the wiser! Carrie thought. *In a couple of months Mrs. Frane will be playing shuffleboard in Florida, and I'll be running my own shop and making enough to buy her out one day. Once I steal Mr. Dobbs's customers, I'll have no problem making payments.*

There was a short break for the judges to discuss the entries and make their decision. The audience was treated to coffee and dessert provided by several of the contributing cafés, and a table was set up with pies and cakes for sale. Carrie mingled with the proprietors of the local businesses, and received a huge amount of compliments for her poem.

"Oh, there you are," said Mrs. Frane. "I guess that was one of those free verse poems you read. Didn't think I'd go for that type of thing, but I have to admit it got to me. Don't know what it meant, but I liked the words just fine. I know if I were the judge you'd win hands down. You're getting closer and closer to becoming *Retro's* owner. You go girl, like they say! Old Mr. Snyder is over on the other side of the room talking with that miserable woman from the library, so I just gave him a nod of the head. I see Mr. Dobbs showed up too. He's back there at the refreshment table with a new lady friend. I guess Miss Mini-Skirt Peppercorn gave him the boot!"

"Oh, don't worry about him. I really appreciate your being here today," Carrie said.

"He probably regrets not keeping company with me, but now it's too late, although I might go over and say hello... never hurts to be polite."

Carrie had stopped listening to Mrs. Frane because Professor McArt was walking back to the microphone.

"Thank you all for participating in our first annual National Poetry Month Competition. I want to thank our generous sponsors for contributing to the winning purse. Let's all try to frequent their businesses to show our appreciation, and support our local shops. I see many of you have already purchased cakes and pies, and that money will be buying essentials to send to our troops overseas.

Now, please ladies and gentlemen, take your seats as I'm about to announce the final decision and the winner of the five-thousand dollar award. But before we begin, I have a brief statement to make. I wasn't quite honest when I said we had three judges for this contest. I am very proud to announce that as a surprise we have a former poet laureate who has come out of retirement. He's been living way up north for years, and he decided to come back to Devon to head up our poetry department here at Hampshire. He is our fourth judge today, and before he presents the winner with the check, he will read from his book, *Wings of Poetry*. Please help me welcome Professor Lawrence Rose."

Carrie's mouth dropped open. She was trapped and had no escape plan. After Professor Rose read from his book, she took a deep breath and turned to search out Mrs. Frane in the audience. Carrie scanned the room and saw her sitting next to Mr. Dobbs. The owner of *Retro & More* wore a frown, and had both thumbs turned down.

Epilogue: Except for the sharp-witted Mrs. Frane and Professor Rose, no one else seemed to notice the similarity in Carrie's poem to the ones that the professor read from his book, perhaps because he'd chosen those that had the least amount of comparison to *Collage*. Apparently, after reading her entry, he decided not to make a public display of Carrie's dishonestly and because he gave the lowest possible score to her poem, it canceled out her winning, and the prize went to an ecstatic Eric Willis.

Professor Rose motioned for Carrie to join him at a small corner table where he admonished her for not using original material. She explained her circumstances, which he sympathized with, but told her that it was no reason for cheating. He asked her what she thought she could do to make amends, and that would dissuade him from reporting her. She offered to tutor students, free of charge, who were lagging behind in their business courses. Carrie begged him to let her stay on at Beacon, and at *Second Chance,* and not to tell her parents. She knew her odds of taking over Mrs.

Frane's shop were zero. He agreed upon the condition that she use her own poetry for any future contests, and asked that she email some of her original work to him.

Professor Rose was empathetic to Carrie's situation and her youth, and let her off with a stiff warning. She dried her tears, and gave him a brief hug before joining Eric to congratulate him on his win.

The woman with Mr. Dobbs turned out to be his sister, and after the three chatted, he invited Mrs. Frane to the Spring Fling church dance. Eventually, they joined forces business wise, and domestically, and became snowbirds, wintering in St. Augustine and spending the warmer months in Devon. Mrs. Frane, now Mrs. Dobbs, eventually forgave Carrie and the two hired her to manage *Second Chance*. Mrs. Frane sold *Retro & More*, whose location had inexplicably become the latest hot spot, to Mr. Dobbs's sons, who turned it into a popular bed and breakfast.

The budding May-December romance between Mr. Snyder and Miss Peppercorn escalated to his proposal of marriage, which she accepted. They purchased a home on four beautifully wooded acres in the countryside, and now spend their spare time fostering rescue dogs.

Carrie's folks did well, but decided to stay put in the neighboring town of Bedford where they'd made many new friends. They visited their daughter on weekends, and after Carrie received her Masters from Hampshire, she became Mrs. Eric Willis.

WRITER'S CRAMP

"**D**ear Ms. Malone, or may I call you Mindy? Let me be the first to congratulate you on the spectacular manuscript you recently submitted. I have rarely seen such fine work, even from well-published, seasoned authors. I feel sure your endeavor will make you as famous (and wealthy!) as J.K. Rowling. We are the only traditional publishing house that doesn't require an agent to represent you. Our staff is prepared to make you an extremely generous offer. Just sign on the dotted line below, so that we may send you an enormous advance. It has…"

I felt a heavy arm fling across my chest waking me from my dream of dreams. I opened my eyes to see my ever-present boyfriend, Doug, a restless sleeper, making a U-turn in bed, disturbing me in the process. We'd lived together in my one-bedroom apartment for the past eight months, in which time he had quit his job because the boss hadn't taken his advice over a small matter, and managed to use up a good portion of my savings, promising to pay me back as soon as business picked up…meaning when he got a job. I knew I should have looked for a roommate who could actually pay half the rent, but Doug had swept me off my feet.

My parents knew nothing of this live-in arrangement, and certainly wouldn't have been in favor of it. Luckily, they were tucked away in a small town in Massachusetts, and on the rare occasions that they visited Manhattan, I managed to meet them downstairs in the lobby. My brothers, all four of them, were older than I was and had settled with their families in and around the beautiful New England town of Williamsburg.

I kept most of my relationship with Doug a secret from my family, and Mom and Dad were in no rush to marry me off. Mom ran a cozy inn adjacent to the fashionable one at Flower Hill, and Dad was a couples' counselor who had seen too many marriages headed south, although he'd managed to save more than the ones that ended in divorce. He'd always advised me to wait until I was a hundred percent sure and never to settle. I mentioned that I was dating someone, but it wasn't serious yet, which seemed to satisfy them. Thank goodness they both led busy lives and didn't meddle in mine!

I had been raised to believe in the sanctity of marriage, but at the ripe old age of twenty-eight, and surrounded by beautiful, stylish young women in New York, I'd hoped that Doug would end up being the man of my dreams, and not the guy interrupting them. Unfortunately, Doug said he had no interest in marriage and laughed at what he called my old-fashioned values, the ones I'd always been proud of before I met him. It was a mistake letting him move in with me, but I felt he'd change his views about marriage once he saw how compatible we were and how much better his life would be with me in it. It could happen, right?

I'd met Doug Patterson and his friend, Arthur Dekker, at The Holy Cow, where I've worked for the last five years as one of their servers. The Cow, as we called it, was a vegetarian restaurant and juice bar where I could always make patrons laugh by promising that the wheat grass had just been mowed and the tofu freshly caught. Both of the guys joked around with me, and since Arthur was wearing a wedding band, I ended up with Doug, who had no problem being openly flirtatious. As soon as Arthur excused himself to take a call from his wife (cell phone usage was discouraged at The Cow), Doug asked me out and I agreed.

I'd been in the process of interviewing potential roommates when Doug suggested that he move in with me. It seemed like a good idea at the time, but it caused major disruption in my apartment on Jane Street in Greenwich Village. Although I was a waitress, my goal was to be a published author. I'd been writing since I was twelve years old and was eager for a change in careers before I hit thirty. My home office, which consisted of a wooden plank on top of two battered file cabinets, had fit nicely in the corner of the only bedroom, but since Doug wasn't working for the moment he'd started sleeping late and my typing irritated him. He and Arthur transferred my setup into the living room, which was already overcrowded with his junk. Whenever I started to object, he'd put some new move on me and with a sigh, I'd dismiss the six cartons marked "Doug's Stuff" and submit. Chemistry can be a dangerous word.

Submit was a familiar word to me. I'd surrounded myself

with every writer's magazine and instruction book learning how to submit my manuscripts for publication. There were so many rules and guidelines, and until recently many required a self-addressed, stamped envelope for a reply. I was convinced that the publishers were steaming off the stamps for their personal use since half of them never came back to me with a yes, no, maybe, or what were you thinking? Lately there were plenty of agents and publishing houses that had switched to email, but I felt more secure sending in my work through snail mail hoping it had more of a chance than a cyber version, which could easily be deleted.

I was used to getting up early, having breakfast and writing until noon, and then heading off to my job at the restaurant, sometimes for a double shift. Doug wasn't thrilled with the arrangement because he disliked the smell of coffee waking him, which interfered with his much-needed nine hours of sleep. He'd finally started interviewing with some advertising agencies, and although they didn't seem to be interested in him, Doug wanted to be lively and fresh in case they changed their minds. He was beginning to cramp my style and one rum-soaked evening, I gave him a goodbye speech. He turned the lights down low, lunged for me and got a reprieve. There were times I thought he was Satan incarnate leading me down the wrong path, but I knew the fault was due to my own insecurities.

The morning that I was jarred out of my acceptance dream was the first time in years I couldn't think of anything to write. I was blocked. Who would ever publish me now? I had kept all the form letters and emails turning down my work, and fantasized that one day my executive secretary (recommended by Stephen King) would send off my own form letters to those cruel places saying "na na na na na na—you lost out!"

Who cared if Ernest Hemingway wallpapered his living

room with rejection letters, as the story went. This was the twenty-first century and I was tired of working in a restaurant. I couldn't even afford a fresh coat of paint.

I left the apartment without eating for fear of waking sleeping beauty. I needed fresh air to awaken my own senses, and stopped in at a local doughnut shop for coffee and a cruller. I was already overweight, and needed those calories and sugar like a hole in the head, but sweets were my reward for failure. While I sat dunking and nibbling, I began to cry. Not tiny tears mind you, but big, wretchedly loud sobs. Oh, I know what you're thinking: that a handsome, unmarried publisher tried to calm me down and insisted on reading the copy in the notebook I always carry with me. Then he'd propose marriage and offer me a contract, in that order. Only it didn't happen that way. The store manager, who looked all of about twelve years old, came over and said I was disturbing his other customers. What was this? The Ritz? No one was spending more than a buck and a half, and they couldn't stomach a few tears? I left with yet another rejection.

When I returned to the apartment, Doug was sitting down to a late breakfast of two toasted sesame bagels topped with whatever leftover cream cheese I'd scored for free at the restaurant. The seeds were all over the place and he said, "Hi Mindy, where have you been hiding? I had to defrost these bagels all by myself, and you know I'm not good at using the microwave. Oh, yeah, the Keurig's on the blink again."

That was it. Doug had to go. Since I was in no mood for romance that morning and he was already dressed in the three-piece suit he'd charged to my account, the timing, for once in my life, was perfect.

"Doug, I don't think this relationship is working out any more. It's not you, it's me." I'd seen a *Seinfeld* rerun with that bit, and it wasn't bad on such short notice. "I'm sure Arthur will put you up till you find your own place. Could you please plan on moving out today?"

He sidled up to me and began to nudge into my ample hips, but I was adamant. Doug knew his hours were numbered. He called Arthur, telling him (loudly) what a needy loser I was, and then packed.

"For your information, I have a job interview this morning, which I'm going to nail, and you could have been the hot babe who'd take the ride with me. You're making a big mistake, and you'll regret it once you're on the market again," he said, getting ready to depart.

Did he seriously call me a hot babe? I didn't know if I should be flattered or infuriated, but yelled, "I'm not a piece of meat!" and slammed the door after him.

I dragged my desk, piece by piece, back into the bedroom, changed the sheets and dressed for work, Doug's final words stinging in my ears.

I got to The Cow a little early and ran into Alissa Frank, an aspiring actress and my best friend, who worked there as the hostess.

"Hey, Mindy, glad you're on the schedule today. I have some good news for you. Remember that piece you wrote about a health food restaurant when you first started working here? A bunch of us are going over to an open mike night down at that big church on Hudson. It's a mixed bag of poetry, monologues—you know, stuff like that. You could read your essay. I bet everyone would love it. It's a popular place and you never know who's going to show up."

"I only hope Doug doesn't make an appearance. We are so over. I kicked his unemployed butt out this morning. Never should have let that happen in the first place," I said, trying to sound tough, yet holding back tears of possible regret.

"Aw, it's for the best. That guy was never going to propose. Why waste your time and what's wrong with being single for a few more years? What's the rush? Don't forget, you always have me as your guide and mentor, so if you come tonight I promise I won't let you walk off with another player. A lot of nice people will be there. It's free entertainment and refreshments, plus a chance for us to perform and get feedback. The church does request a suggested donation of whatever you can afford. Mostly everyone gives a few bucks although I've seen tens and twenties in the basket. It goes to a food bank for seniors in the area," Alissa said. "I emailed an agent I know and asked him to come. I think he may be interested in taking me on as a client."

Alissa could have played the gorgeous, tall, thin and talented best friend of the everything-challenged girl (me) in any chick-flick movie. She was always trying to get me to work out with her, but who had time? Apparently, she did and had no trouble keeping her wraith-like figure. I wasn't jealous...well, maybe a little.

"You've sold me," I said, my tears drying up, "but I still can't believe you said 'mixed bag.' What is this, the eighties?"

"See, you have a real flair for comedy. Now get your apron on and serve those upper east-siders and millennials who ventured down to the village today," she said, and after a brief "thank you BFF I love you" hug, I got down to business.

I had almost forgotten about a piece called "But Is It Healthy?" that I'd written several years ago. It was a cute bit about customers in a health food restaurant asking their server, who lived on cheeseburgers and fries, to explain the difference between the two rice milks on the menu, how much soy was in the ersatz meatloaf, and what brand of quinoa was used. The server has to make up answers because she wouldn't eat that junk if they gave it to her on a silver platter. I had given copies to my boss and the staff, and they'd all enjoyed it. Let's see who else would agree with them. I'd find out tonight after The Cow closed. Without Doug to take care of at home, I began to look forward to a night out.

Later that evening Alissa read her monologue and the small crowd, made up of fellow performers, family and friends, applauded and cheered. There were a few singers, some slam poetry, and then it was my turn. I hadn't memorized my piece as the others had, and after clearing my throat about ninety times I began to read. Alissa had been right. Everyone laughed and clapped for what seemed an unusually long time, and I thanked them all for being so supportive.

The pastor took over the mike and I sat down, smiling and happy. No matter how many rejection letters I had in my files, I was going to continue writing.

"Okay folks," said Pastor Grenville, "that was one of the best collections we've ever had at open mike night. Hope to see you all next Tuesday. I want to thank those of you who were able to make contributions. I can assure you that a lot of people in our area will be well nourished because of your generosity since we've begun this program. There's coffee and a sheet cake my wife baked for tonight, so enjoy and God bless you all."

I'd eaten lunch when I first arrived at The Cow, but it had been so busy later on that I didn't have a chance for a quick dinner bite, and was now starving. I knew I shouldn't have cake, but I'd limit my serving to one small piece. Or two.

Mrs. Pastor, as everyone called her, joined us and brought in a ginormous platter of cut up fruit and set it next to the cake. I helped her serve and kept a portion of the fruit for myself, deciding, for once, to skip the cake. Now that Doug wasn't in my life anymore I could probably find at least twenty minutes in the morning to do some speed-walking.

"Mindy, I want you to meet someone. Pete Garson, this is my dearest friend Mindy Malone. She works at The Cow with me, but she's going to be a famous writer one day," said my publicist, Alissa.

"Nice to meet you. I enjoyed your essay, Mindy. Excuse me ladies, I need to speak to someone before she leaves," Pete said, and took off like a shot.

"Gee Alissa, was it something I said, or didn't say? Oh, I see. He's over there talking to the Marilyn Monroe looka-like. They do make a gorgeous couple," I said, trying to hold in my stomach and wishing I'd worn my discount store wannabe Spanx.

"Don't get your leggings in a knot," she said, mixing metaphors or creating a new one, "he's the agent I told you about. That's why he comes to open mike. I've asked him to represent me, and if he liked my monologue he might consider taking me on for some legit theater work. He's seen me in a few off-off Broadway productions, so may-be after tonight I'll move up a notch. Lose one of those 'offs.' Be right back, bestie, I need a coffee refill. You want anything?"

"No thanks. I'm good with the fruit," I said, watch-ing her flit away wondering how she could maneuver that quickly on five inch stilettos. I decided to take a sly glance over Pete's way and instead found myself gazing into his marbled hazel eyes.

"Sorry about my abrupt departure before, but I wanted to give Marilyn over there my card. I think I can get some work for her," Pete said. "Where's Alissa? Hang around be-cause I have some good news for her. I'd like to represent her. We've discussed it in the past and I'll take the chance. I'd like to be able to get her into a couple of auditions for some off-Broadway productions because she can sing and dance as well as act."

Of course, she can.

"Did I hear my name?" Alissa said, juggling a cup of coffee and an enormous slab of cake.

Dear Lord in Heaven, I know I'm not supposed to pray for small insignificant things, but could you please take five or ten pounds off me and maybe add it to Alissa? She won't even notice it, but it'd be a good jumpstart to my diet. Amen.

"Yes, you did," Pete said. "Uh, Mindy, you okay? Can I get you a glass of water?"

I realized I'd momentarily taken leave of my senses asking for the impossible.

"Nope, I'm fine with coffee," I said, although I hadn't taken any. "I mean fruit. Now, what were you saying?"

After Pete and Alissa shook hands on their deal she asked to be excused so that she could share the news with the Pastor, and thank him for making all this possible.

"I'm happy for her," I said, meaning it. "She's so beautiful and talented." I left out the skinny part.

"That she is, but you're no slouch in that department either," he said.

I guess he meant talented because he asked if I'd written anything else.

I mentioned a few novels in my stash, most recently a romance that I felt merited a rewrite. The first version had been submitted and turned down by over a dozen publishers and agents. I hadn't done much work on it since Doug came into my life.

"Maybe it needs a little tweaking," he said. "Mind if I have a look at it? I don't work with writers, but I have a good friend who has a start-up publishing company and he's looking for fresh new authors. Why don't you give me a call and we'll set up an appointment in my office."

He handed me his card and said goodnight as I stood there in shock.

I woke up early the next morning, happy to be back to my old schedule, and considered the offer Pete had made the previous evening. It was time for me to do as much for myself as possible. Doug was out of my life, and the only romance I cared about was in my book. I left a message at Pete's office, opened my laptop, and went to work.

Pete had mentioned tweaking, but when I pulled up and skimmed through the manuscript, I decided it needed major resuscitation. C.P.R., in fact. It was almost as if a giant sea pod had taken over my thoughts and added gratuitous sex, gore and violence to the story. Yes, there was a romantic theme to the novel, but why had I found it necessary to add elements that had never appealed to me in books, or movies? Were our modern-day tastes so influenced by off-color language and low-class behavior that I felt pressured to include it? I realized that I had been trying to fit into a niche that was distasteful to me, and where I didn't belong. I couldn't blame Doug because he'd never asked to read anything of mine.

Pete called my cell that afternoon and we made an appointment for the following week.

Dear Lord, please guide me in writing a decent novel. I don't care if this book ever gets published; I just don't want to be ashamed of it.

Although I had used a slew of curse words in the original manuscript and had included some graphic sex scenes, at least I'd not taken the Lord's name in vain. I'd seen too much of that in e-books I'd downloaded while doing research. It had been offensive not only to me, but obviously to scores of reviewers that I'd canvassed. I didn't want to be a part of that club. For the next few days I did what I thought was a decent rewrite for my story and printed it out, including a full synopsis for Pete to review.

The day of my meeting with Pete, I didn't bother dressing up since I had to go to work afterward, but was sorry I hadn't at least put on a dab of makeup when I saw Pete's office and the handsome suit that he probably paid for by himself. His secretary poured coffee for us from an elegant china pot into matching cups, and not a mug with Doug's chiropractor's name on it like I used at home. Pete and I discussed the manuscript I'd brought with me and his suggestions on how to make it more marketable. We shook hands although I had the feeling he would have been happier giving me a little hug. Pete was single and certainly attractive, but I had made a decision not to get involved with anyone romantically until after my career was underway. I knew I was projecting into the stratosphere because why would Pete be interested in dating me?

A few days later, he called.

"Mindy, I had time to read the entire manuscript and I think you have a great story line. It could be of interest to Phil Gaines, one of the editors over at the publishing startup I told you about. Fuller House. I've made a few notes, but overall it reads smoothly. I'm booked in the office for the rest of the day, so why don't we meet for dinner?" he said.

When I came out of my trance, I thanked Pete for his input and said I was free after work. He mentioned a restaurant that was only a few blocks from The Cow and we agreed on a time. I decided to dress up a bit and since I had pretty decent legs; I threw a short silk dress and a pair of sling-back heels into my tote bag before leaving the house. I worked my long hair into a messy bun, the style of the moment, and got it right on the first try. A little blush, lipstick, and mascara, and I was ready to greet the world, and hopefully a book deal.

At eight-fifteen that evening, I walked over to the Gotham Restaurant. I took a seat at the bar and ordered a Bloody Mary. Pete came in and apologized for being what seemed to be thirty seconds late before the captain led us to a primo table. We discussed my book and his notes, which clearly would improve the story. I'd been involved in various critique groups over the years, which had been helpful, but Pete's advice made me want to leave the table and hop onto my computer. Well, not really.

"Let me know when you finish the final draft. Then put together a book proposal and I'll introduce you to Phil. There's a growing market in inspirational or good, old-fashioned clean fiction these days. People are getting back to basics and a decent morality, and your book fits right in. I'm pretty sure Fuller House will agree," he said, pushing a stray tendril of my hair back behind my ear.

"Pete, I'm so grateful," I said, trying not to gasp at his delicate touch. "Even if the book doesn't get picked up, I appreciate your going to bat for me. And I agree with what you said. My own values got a little muddled a while back and I put my career on hold. Maybe that's why I was having trouble with my storyline. The first manuscript was anything but inspirational. I'd be mortified if anyone read it."

Pete nodded, and said, "Alissa tells me you're not seeing your boyfriend anymore. Is there anyone else in your life?"

The change in subject floored me. I recouped quickly to say I wasn't sure if I was ready to date at the moment because I was totally focused on my career.

"Can't you have both, Mindy?"

"Not right now, Pete. It's a little complicated. I just got out of an unhealthy relationship. I think I need a break."

"I won't press the point," Pete said. "Please remember that I'm interested in more than just your manuscript."

On any other planet I wouldn't have turned him down, but I wasn't ready to flirt with disaster by rushing into a relationship here on earth.

We sipped our espressos and shared a rich, creamy dessert, not like the chewy brown rice pudding with goat's milk I was used to serving. He walked me home and said goodnight with the same handshake we'd used in his office.

Pete and Phil must have been really good buddies, because Fuller House accepted my reformatted book in a minimum amount of time. It did fairly well for a breakout novel from an unknown, or the term I preferred, emerging author, but I held on to my waitressing job to help fill the financial dent that Doug had made in my account. My former boyfriend and I no longer had any personal contact, but lately he'd been paying back what he owed me with weekly checks, so I assumed he'd found employment.

I continued to write every day and Pete called weekly to see if anything else was near completion, even an outline. He'd told me over our occasional lunch that it would be a good idea to have a second book in the making. Our relationship remained businesslike. I knew that Fuller House was beginning to offer contracts to their popular authors for writing one or two more books a year, but I was too new at the game to hope for that. In any case, I'd started a new manuscript, although it wasn't exactly rolling along. The truth was I didn't even have a working title.

A month or so later, Pete called and asked if he could stop by after work. He had some exciting news that he wanted to tell me about in person. I had an early shift that day at The Cow and told him any time after five would be fine.

"I'm going to throw on some spaghetti later and you're welcome to join me," I said, wanting to thank him with more than words for all he'd done for me. I wasn't much of a cook, but who doesn't like pasta? I was at my laptop when Pete arrived with chilled champagne and caviar.

"Wow," I said, accepting his offerings and feeling mortified about what I was going to serve him. "What's the occasion?"

"Congratulations, Mindy," Pete said, "you have a contract for your second, and hopefully third book, if you want it. I had lunch with Phil today, and he told me he was going to discuss it with you. I asked if he minded if I gave you the news."

I was trying to get over the word contract and my name in the same sentence, but managed to shake my head in agreement.

"That is awesome! How can I ever thank you," I said, taking a sip of the champagne he'd poured.

"He'll call you in the morning to set up a meeting to iron out the details. I have an attorney on staff who'll be able to look over the contract, but it's probably clear cut. These are honest guys. I hope you don't mind that you heard it from me instead of Phil," he said.

"Of course, I don't mind. Without you I'd be nowhere," I said, hoping I could move at warp speed on the new book now that I had a major incentive from Fuller House.

"I don't believe that. I just helped move the process along. And lucky for you that your book fits the current popular genre," Pete said, while I silently thanked the Lord for steering me in the right direction. "Now, what have you got to go with that spaghetti?"

"I usually dump some jarred tomato sauce on top and finish it off with grated cheese," I said, embarrassed that I hadn't prepared something more special for the evening.

"I think I can do a little better than that," he said. "Do you mind?"

Why would I mind anything this man suggested? Pete was surely my bearer-of-good-news archangel, Gabriel.

I set the table and thirty minutes later we sat down to an impressive meal. After looking through the sparse offerings in my fridge, Pete managed to put together an unusual, but delicious pasta dish with chopped eggs, sliced scallions, and a chunk of butter the size of Wisconsin. He topped it off with some of the caviar he'd brought along, and we enjoyed a five-star dinner.

When he left that evening, I reluctantly extended my hand for our usual shake. He seemed even more hesitant to do the same, but when our hands finally touched, it sent shivers from my shoulders down to the soles of my feet.

"Are you going to let go?" he said.

"Not unless I have to," I said, barely able to breathe.

He drew me close and we kissed. When we finally pulled apart, he said, "I'm glad we were friends first, Mindy. We have a lot of talking to do, and not only about your books. I'll call you tomorrow. Good night."

After Pete left, I cued up my iPod and did my version of a happy dance around the living room, and then cleaned the kitchen. I prayed before I got into bed and thanked God for the blessings that had come my way. I could take care of the silly stuff myself. The dancing had been fun and therapeutic, and maybe if I did that in the evenings and walked most mornings before I turned on my laptop, those extra pounds would melt away.

I climbed into bed and fell into an easy sleep. When I awoke the next morning, I went back to work on my new novel, *Friends First*.

My second book didn't make the bestsellers list either, but six months after it was published and a third in the making, I was able to quit my job at The Cow and become a full-time writer. I donated a dozen copies of my print books to the church gift shop, and they were pleased that a now-steady parishioner slash novelist was part of their congregation.

Doug managed to pay back every penny he had borrowed, and even came to my book signings. Although we were no longer romantically linked, we were able to put the past behind us to become friends. Alissa's career had taken off after Pete became her agent and whenever we were free, she and I went to the church's open mike nights. It was only a couple of years after our first night there that we had each realized our dream. It was gratifying to be able to leave more than the five dollars we initially had to scrape together for the collection basket.

"My Dear Mrs. Garson: Although we are only in the second year of our new five-year contract, I must inform you that we can no longer represent you. Your previous books did well, but we have no interest in your new outline. We have told you over and over that our readers are not interested in married love or the mush you've been sending in. I strongly suggest that you go back to Fuller House where you belong…"

I woke up, this time with a jab in my stomach. The baby was kicking again. I rolled over to my sleeping husband, but decided not to wake him. I'd tell Pete about the dream in the morning.

THIS WILL ALL BE YOURS

"Lucy, is Eddie back yet? I could use some help downstairs," Harry said, wiping away the sweat from his brow.

"No, Mr. Brite, haven't seen him," said Lucy, who'd worked for years as one of the grocery store's cashiers. Eddie was supposed to be back from the bank by two, but Lucy knew he'd be late as usual. Eddie had enough energy for a lot of things, but working wasn't one of them.

And poor old Mr. Brite, Lucy thought, *lifting those twenty pound sacks of rice and flour at his age. Why, it's a wonder he hasn't given himself a heart attack. Eddie does the least amount of work with the most amount of commotion to make himself look busy. How the boss doesn't see that is amazing!*

"Please let me know when he gets here. I'll be down in the basement taking inventory," Harry said.

"Will do, Mr. Brite. I'd come help you myself, but I can't leave my station. It's almost five and we'll get plenty busy any minute," Lucy said. "Last-minute shoppers and all."

Harry Brite and his wife, Gail, were the owners of Brite Brothers Grocery. The couple had taken in their nephew, Edward, after his parents were killed in a car accident. Eddie's dad was Harry's beloved younger brother, and not a day went by that Harry didn't think about him and miss their camaraderie. The two brothers had worked together for over twenty years without a cross word between them.

Harry and Gail adopted Eddie after the accident when the boy was only eight years old. His aunt and uncle, who were already in their forties, raised him and treated him like the child they were never able to have. Although Eddie called them his aunt and uncle, the Brites thought of him as their son.

When Eddie finished high school, Gail was no longer needed at home in the afternoons to make sure he did his homework, so fulfilling a lifelong dream, she opened up a boutique on Woodfield Street, an upscale busy thoroughfare in their small town. Gail, who consistently dressed in chic, flattering outfits, had a keen sense of fashion, which served her well when selecting an eclectic grouping of women's clothing, shoes and accessories for her store. Many of her friends, who'd always admired her style, became customers and once the word was out, women in neighboring villages added to the clientele.

That had been over a decade ago, and since his high school graduation Eddie had worked in his uncle's grocery store, although some of the other employees were loath to agree that it was actual work.

Brite Brothers was one of the original stores that had

been built on Oak Street and had been in business for over seventy years. Harry was proud of the fact that the interior had never been changed. Except for a few minor repairs, and the addition of updated scanners and a sprinkler system, everything was exactly the way it was when his great-grandfather ran it. Harry refused to replace the old, wooden-plank floors with tile as so many of the modern markets did. He liked the look of a freshly scrubbed family-owned store with handwritten signs denoting the weekly specials.

Gail had suggested that Eddie attend a community college in the neighborhood, but because his high school record for those all important junior and senior years was poor, it would have been a stretch for him to be accepted, and his application was turned down.

"Don't fret about college right now. I'd rather he works with me for a year, and then maybe he'll get more serious about his studies. He can always apply later, and don't forget, work experience accounts for a lot these days," Harry said. "Let's not push the boy into something he's not ready for."

"I'm going to agree with you under one condition. He's to work in the store whenever you're there," Gail said. "I don't like you putting in those long hours at your age, and one of these days you'll need to retire and who else is there to leave the business to? That's what we've planned for, and it's what your brother would have wanted. The more Eddie knows about the day-to-day dealings, the more prepared he'll be when that day comes. He can always take some college courses in the evening or online."

"Why don't we discuss it with him?" Harry said. "I think it's a sound plan. And you're right; Brite Brothers can continue to prosper after I'm gone. I might even add 'and Son' to the sign outside."

Eddie jumped at the chance to forgo trying to get into another college even though it meant putting in at least forty hours a week to work with his uncle. He lived at home with Harry and Gail because even with his inflated salary, he couldn't find a place that would be as spacious as his present accommodations, which were rent-free. Eddie had taken over the large, finished basement of their house and often had friends stop by. Gail, who had a tender spot for her only nephew, had made his quarters comfortable and to his credit, Eddie never took advantage by playing loud music or allowing visitors to smoke or drink alcohol. He went to church with his adoptive parents every Sunday, and made sure to add something to the collection plate. All in all, the threesome got along quite well.

Eddie, at age twenty-eight, had grown into a handsome man, who'd inherited his dad's thick, wavy, reddish-brown hair, and deep-amber-colored eyes. He casually dated different young women from the neighborhood, but was determined not to settle down with anyone until his fortune was made and that's where all his energy was being spent.

Harry loved his nephew even though he was well aware of Eddie's faults, and paid him more than he was worth in order to pique the boy's interest in moving up the ladder.

"This will all be yours one day, son," Harry told him. "You've got to learn the business from the bottom up. That's why I have you stocking shelves and cleaning floors, so you'll know how to manage others when the time comes."

For the first few years, Eddie followed his uncle around and showed a keen ability for customer service. He suggested new products that he knew to be popular, and was rarely wrong. He drove to work with Harry and they left together in the evening. Gail was usually home in time to have a hot meal waiting for them, or the three would go out to local restaurants and catch up on the day's events. The family genuinely cared about each other, and Eddie did his best to manipulate them in a kindly manner.

Unfortunately, for the last six months there had been a noticeable change in Eddie's behavior. The young man had a good heart, but there was no denying how lazy he'd become. When he'd turned eighteen, his aunt and uncle had bought him a used car. Harry didn't want Eddie to be bogged down with car payments and had encouraged him to save his money for a rainy day. Now in his twenties, Eddie no longer rode to the store with his uncle, and no matter how many times Harry chided him about coming in late or leaving early, Eddie could always wheedle himself back into his uncle's good graces.

Anyone who read the local papers knew that a huge real estate conglomerate, Leonard Developers, was buying up properties on Oak Street. The once-thriving block of Mom and Pop businesses would become extinct, and rebuilt as home to a modern lifestyle shopping mall if the developers had their way. A few of the business owners, mainly those ready to retire with no one to take over, had already sold off their stores, or were compensated for the balance of their leases. The developers had razed the small buildings and held the land for expansion.

Eddie hoped that it was only a matter of time before his uncle followed suit. He knew there were big bucks involved, and he'd convince his aunt and uncle to give him a share.

"Hey Unc, why don't you sell the business to Leonard's?" he said, as though the previously thought out idea had just popped into his head. They were dining in a local Italian restaurant, and he'd waited until the carafe of Chianti was empty before bringing up the subject. "They'll give you a great price so you and Aunt Gail can retire. I mean, Aunt Gail could still have her boutique and you could even help out there if you're bored. With the extra money, you guys could buy a summer home, some place nice at the beach, and not worry about an outdated business."

"Honey, Eddie does have a point. You're working so hard when you should be thinking about retiring in a couple of years. My store practically runs itself, but you could go on buying trips with me, or take over the bookkeeping. You know that's not my strong suit," Gail said, finishing her wine.

"Unc, most of the folks already go up to the highway to the big markets anyway. We can't compete with those prices."

"We may not be able to match their prices, but they simply can't match the quality of our meats, our produce and the specialized canned goods. Even our bakery, although small, is top-notch, and we can hardly keep enough of our own coffee blend in stock what with all the restaurants buying it as well as our customers. There's nothing wrong with hard work; it's what's made this country great. Aunt Gail and I always wanted you to take over one day. How many of your friends can say that they'll step into a going business and be their own boss?" Harry said, ignoring his wife's proposal. "Son, this will all be yours. Now, if we can get back to dinner, I'd like to order dessert and a cup of Brite Brothers coffee!"

Little did Harry Brite suspect that his nephew had no interest in taking over the market. Eddie knew the big money was in selling it to the developers while they were still offering top dollar. The Brites had no one else to leave their money to except him, not that he wished them any ill will because they'd been loving and generous to him since the day his parents died, but he had no intention of working the daily grind if he could avoid it.

But business was business. Harry owned the one-story building that housed Brite Brothers, and notwithstanding the dated interior, Leonard's had told Eddie it'd be worth approximately half a million if the deal could be brokered quickly. Both men knew the real estate was way more valuable than the building, which would be knocked down, and the land would be added to the mall space. Harry was a well-respected entrepreneur in the community and if he agreed to sell, Eddie knew the remaining shop owners would cave in.

Eddie had been secretly meeting with Stuart Leonard, one of the partners of the company, and assured him that Harry would sell. He had to make that happen. No way did he want to work in a grocery for the rest of his life, even if he owned it. If he could get Harry to sell, they'd all be set for life and whatever his aunt and uncle didn't spend during their lifetime would be left to him. He'd been speaking separately to Harry and Gail, hoping to play one against the other until they both agreed that selling would be beneficial to everyone. Gail wasn't opposed to the idea, but since Harry's family had started the business decades ago, the final decision had to be left up to her husband.

Lucy admired her boss for not selling out to the developers who'd been coming around looking to buy up all the properties on Oak Street. A few of the smaller businesses had already accepted the deals presented to them, but at a recent town hall meeting Harry and a bunch of other entrepreneurs, who'd been neighbors for years, decided to sit tight and run their shops the old fashioned way. Harry wanted to carry on his family's tradition of good food at fair prices, with personalized service to his customers.

While Harry was in the basement in the midst of the

work his nephew should have been doing, Eddie sauntered in just as Lucy was ringing up Mrs. Gomez, her last customer before closing out her register for the day.

"Hello there, Mrs. Gomez. How are the kids?" Eddie said.

"We're all fine. Thank you for asking. Nice to see you, Eddie. Thanks, Lucy. Tell Mr. Brite hello for me and that the peaches were as delicious as promised. Good night, all," Mrs. Gomez said.

"Please let me take those groceries to your car," Eddie said, grabbing both bags with one hand. "A beautiful woman like you shouldn't be carrying heavy packages."

"Eddie, you are a flirt and I'm a married woman," she said, with a winning smile. "But I do appreciate it. I'm parked right out back."

"Oh, you're a charmer, all right," Lucy said, when Eddie returned to the store. "But how about giving me a hand with those end-cap shelves? They need restocking because we have a big sale going on this weekend and I'd like to be out of here by six. Your uncle's doing inventory so we're closing up early tonight."

"Okay, Lucy, let me finish my lemonade. It's plenty hot out there for this time of year. Where'd you say my uncle was? I want to discuss something with him."

"Where do you think he'd be if he's taking inventory? He's down in the basement, probably sorting out all those jarred sauces. They need to be brought up here after he counts them and that's a heavy load. He was looking for you to lend a hand, but decided to do it himself. Mr. Brite shouldn't be exerting himself like that at his age. It'll be too much for him one day."

"Nah, he's a tough old bird. You go home, Lucy. I'll come in early tomorrow morning and stock those shelves," Eddie said.

"That'll be the day when you walk in here before eleven.

I'll do it myself. You go downstairs and help out your uncle," Lucy said, and slammed shut her register.

"Hi, Uncle Harry, Lucy said you could use some help. What can I do for you?" Eddie said, joining his uncle in the basement stock room.

"I could have used some help an hour or two ago, but it's almost done now. Where were you? I told you I needed a pair of strong arms. I can't do all this myself anymore," Harry said, out of breath as he scolded his nephew.

"I was making a deposit at the bank, like you said for me to do, and I ran into the developers. They asked me if you'd given any more thought to their business deal. I couldn't be rude and walk away. You know, you and Aunt Gail could retire pretty darn well on what they're offering, and you wouldn't have to work so hard," he said, waving his hand at the steel shelving filled with products that lined the basement walls. "And Aunt Gail is busier than ever. Don't you think she deserves a break? She could probably sell her store to the developers also, although they're concentrating on Oak Street right now," Eddie said.

"Aunt Gail is perfectly capable of running her boutique and very happy about it. I wouldn't be working this hard if you'd show up on time. Eddie, this business was good enough for my father and his father, and your dad, so it certainly is good enough for me." Harry loved Eddie and softened his tone. "And don't forget, one day this will all be yours."

Yeah, one day when the new mall's been built and it's too late to get a decent price for this old dump from the developers, Eddie thought.

"Maybe you're right, Unc," Eddie said, wanting to get back into Harry's good graces.

There's gotta be another angle.

When Stuart Leonard met Eddie at the bank earlier that afternoon, he told him that there were only a few days left before the architects would commence their plan for the extended block. Stuart was sure that the remaining small businesses would sell out, particularly since Leonard's had recently upped the buy-out price.

"Eddie," Stuart said, "if we don't have Harry's property within a week, there will be no further offers. We'll simply construct the new lifestyle mall around your uncle's building. I don't have to tell you how ridiculous Brite's will look compared to the modern stores. Everything will be brand spanking new except that old joke of a grocery."

"I've been trying to convince my uncle, but so far, he hasn't budged," Eddie said, upset that he hadn't made any progress with the deal.

"We already own the row of old stores across the street from Brite's. Half of them were empty anyway or on their way out. The owners made out pretty good by taking our offers. We'll be bringing in a major supermarket with its own café, and your uncle's business will fall apart. Right now people have to drive way up to the highway if they want to do a big shopping, but the older folks don't do that because of the distance, but when it's right here in town... you can see the handwriting on the wall," Stuart said. "Your aunt was smart opening that boutique over on Woodfield. We'd never be able to afford to buy out those businesses, for the moment anyway. For whatever reason, Oak Street just doesn't have the draw anymore."

"You gotta give me a little more time. I think my aunt will go along with it. She sees how wiped Harry is when he comes home. When I mentioned that they could get a summer place at the beach with the buy-out, you should have seen her face light up. And she could always keep her boutique, even take on Harry to keep him busy, or partner up with one of her gal pals. I know I can get my uncle to agree, but I need more time. Can you give me another week? I promise I'll work it out," Eddie said.

"You're a sharp guy. I'll give you a full week, but after that it's out of my hands. I got partners to answer to," Stuart said. "You're aware that most of the other hold-outs have given in to our offers. The couple of independent businesses that are left are standing strong, with customers supporting them, like Brite's, but it's not the wave of the future. The town council already rejected a plea to prohibit us from coming in."

"Yeah, Uncle Harry was at that meeting. He came home feeling really depressed," Eddie said, with a touch of empathy in his voice.

"Listen, I understand your uncle's position. That store's been his whole life, but even he has to see what's happened to this side of town," Stuart said. "And I have to say, that your town council is on the ball. They asked if we could incorporate attractive townhouses for the influx of millennials and empty nesters who'll be moving in from the suburbs once we get going. That was going to be the second phase of our building plan anyway, so we agreed. It was a good compromise and everything will be landscaped to perfection. No big ugly signage anywhere. The downtown will be beautiful and well structured, and most important, freshly revitalized. None of these falling down shops with mismatched signs."

"I'll make it happen. You can count on me. My uncle always told me that Brite Brothers would be mine one day, but I simply have no interest in it except for selling it. I bet Uncle Harry would give me some of the money right away to start up a new business here in town, maybe go into commercial real estate to help lease out all the new places you're building. It's not that I don't want to work; I just don't want to be a grocery boy all my life," Eddie said. "I'll call you tomorrow."

After the two men finished the inventory, Harry asked Eddie to stay on and help him clean up.

"I'm feeling a little tired, son. Would you run upstairs to the utility closet and get me that wide broom. You can tell Lucy to take off also. You'll have to bring up these jars when we're done here, so no need to make her wait."

"Sure, Unc, be right back. I'll do the sweeping, and I'll make sure that stuff gets on the shelves for the sale. How about a cold drink from the cooler? You better sit down. You don't look so hot. Do you feel okay? Want me to call Aunt Gail?" Eddie said, concerned that his uncle didn't look his usual vital self.

"Oh, I'm fine. Take more than a day's work to bring me down. Let's get moving so we can go home for dinner. I think I'll have a nice scotch and soda tonight."

When Eddie returned he was shocked to find his Uncle Harry flat on his back and as pale as milk. He called 911, and tried to revive him, but it was too late. Uncle Harry was dead.

He slumped down on a stool next to his uncle and cried. Harry and his wife had been so good to him all these years, and he felt guilty for slacking off during the last few months, his mind only on selling out. Eddie waited for the authorities to arrive, and dialed Gail from his cell phone to break the sad news.

The next few days were busy ones for Harry's widow, and Eddie. After the funeral he got in touch with the developers and told them to draw up the contracts to purchase the property. He knew his uncle had left the business to him. Even though Gail was half-owner in the market, it would have been too much for his aunt to manage along with her boutique. The transfer was just a formality to be settled at the will reading in the lawyer's office two days hence.

Eddie recalled his uncle's words, "one day this will all be yours." Now it would be his to do with as he pleased.

Hey, I'm a good guy, he thought. *I'll take care of Aunt Gail and give her half the money from the sale even if it means less for me. Wait a minute, there's a way I can give myself a bonus. The building is going to be torn down once the developers get their hands on it, so why don't I burn it down first? I'll get the insurance and save Stuart the trouble of flattening it.*

Eddie knew there was a bar in the shady area of town and decided to stop in for a beer. After looking around and chatting up the locals at the pool table, he was able to find two men passing through ready to make a few bucks. They agreed to torch the market and the building, and make it look like an accident. They said they'd done it before, but never stuck around long enough to find out if arson had been suspected. Eddie cautioned them to be extra careful because he couldn't take the chance of an investigation. He okayed the five thousand dollars they asked for to do the job right.

"Now listen up, meet me tomorrow at the store at one o'clock to start rigging the place. Come in the back door because I don't want anyone to see you. We're closed for the next two days out of respect for Uncle Harry, and the employees were invited to the lawyer's office to hear what my uncle left them. The reading of the will is set for two o'clock and I want you guys to start the fire at exactly that time. I'll give you half the money tonight to show good faith and the rest tomorrow when you show up. And then you get out of town."

The three agreed upon the terms, and after hitting up Eddie for another pitcher of beer and a platter of wings, they parted ways.

The next day the two thugs arrived on time to collect their payment. Eddie went over the plan with them once more before leaving for the lawyer's office. After dismantling the ceiling sprinklers, they began to set the ancient gas boiler in the basement to explode at the appointed time. The men were a little dim-witted and didn't realize that by deactivating the sprinklers, they were establishing hard and fast evidence that arson, and not an accident, had felled the grocery. By the time someone called the fire department, it would be too late to save Brite Brothers, and the store would be irreparably damaged. Eddie would later explain that the cost would be exorbitant to restore the market to its former glory, and it would have to be sold to the developers for practicality. When the fire started, Eddie would be far enough away from the market, with witnesses as to his whereabouts. He'd be cleared of any suspicion, and could plan for his future.

Eddie sat next to his Aunt Gail, consoling her, and at two o'clock sharp the lawyer read the provisions of the will. The employees each received two thousand dollars, and could stay on at the grocery until they retired, their pension plans intact. As expected, the house and bank accounts were all held jointly, so Harry's wife wouldn't have to concern herself with finances for her future. They'd lived modestly and their net worth was more than Gail would ever need in her lifetime.

Now it's my turn, Eddie thought. *Once I get the money from Stuart I'll give out extra farewell bonuses to Lucy and the rest of them. Uncle Harry would have wanted that.*

"And to my nephew, Edward Brite, Jr.," the lawyer continued, "I bequeath the Brite Brothers Grocery and property on the following condition. He is to work there for the next two years keeping the business in its present state except for minor repairs. If Edward decides to leave the grocery before the two years are up, or attempts to sell or dispose of it in any manner whatsoever, he will no longer be the beneficiary of Brite's, and the business and property will revert to my estate with Gail Brite as trustee. As I've instructed in this document and previously agreed to by my wife, she will then sell the entire property to Leonard Developers and after expenses, the profits will be donated to the town's local charities."

"Goodness! Look at Eddie," Lucy cried out, "He's slumped over in his chair. He must have passed out hearing the good news!"

LITERARY
LICENSE

It's clear I never should have become involved with Will Viner, but such things often happen to bored middle-aged housewives, particularly when certain husbands remain oblivious to the hours their spouses spend away from home.

When Polly and Piper, our twin daughters, went off to college, my husband and I, Ian and Nina Barnes, decided to stay in our Long Island suburban home and define our newly acquired leisure time.

In June, while the girls were on summer break, they drove up to their grandparents' place in Vermont to enjoy a cooler climate for the season where they'd already found jobs as counselors at a local sleepaway camp. My folks had a cottage on the lake, and it was a fun vacation for all of them.

Ian continued commuting to Manhattan where he was a partner in a small, but successful, accounting firm and on the weekends he was able to devote himself to his longtime hobby of photography with a local camera club. I continued working two days a week for a major publishing company in Long Island City, and decided to join a creative writing class held on Tuesday afternoons in the community room of our village bookstore, The Book Café. Our group, led by Ms. Hannah Fox, was made up of ten housewives. And Will Viner.

Will was your typical bad boy, complete with a long ponytail, a noisy motorcycle, and colorful tattoos that decorated his arms. He had a laundry list of wild stories that commanded the attention from most of the women who met for coffee in the café before class. It wasn't uncommon for Hannah to find us there seated around him, enraptured by his conversation. Will was the guy your mother warned you about, and cautioned you to stay away from if you ever wanted to marry the right man, live in a nice house, go to church, serve the P.T.A., and lead a respectable life. In his early thirties, Will was about ten years younger than the rest of us. Life had obviously slapped him around a bit, but had been kind enough to have left his baby-sweet face intact.

I was forty-two and no longer listened to my mother.

By our third class all the women, including me, had begun to spruce up our appearance—quite a transformation from the first two sessions when faded cut-offs, stretched-out tee shirts, and flip flops made up the dress code. Some of the women now wore short skirts, more makeup, and what do you know, not a gray root in the bunch.

Hannah Fox turned out to be the biggest surprise. Our dumpy, forty-something leader had gone a little nuts by wearing capris so tight that if she had to take them down to pee, she'd probably stumble out of the bathroom with the pants stuck around her knees. Her trashy, neon-colored tank tops revealed cleavage previously hidden under what was beginning to look like a collection of ugly brown smocks. Hannah might have been a lap dancer in another life because she sure knew how to direct her body in Will's direction.

I remember what I was wearing the day it began because my outfit set me apart from the rest. My Armani-look-alike navy pinstripe suit had served me well on an interview that led to my job as an assistant junior editor, the lowest rung on the ladder in the publishing business. The personnel director mentioned how nicely I was dressed and, after looking over my resume, hired me on the spot, even agreeing to my requested part-time schedule.

Meanwhile, back to the suit. I don't know why I wore it that Tuesday afternoon, or why I coaxed my chestnut brown hair into an elaborate French twist, but about an hour into our workshop my phone vibrated with notice of a text. Hannah had suggested that everyone exchange cell numbers in case we wanted to get together during the week to go over the current assignment, but I was surprised to look down in the middle of one of the lessons to see what Will had typed. "Nina, I like classy women." I felt a curious warmth creep up the back of my neck and hoping I was too young to be menopausal, I smiled to indicate that I was accepting the compliment.

After the rest of the class straggled out at the end of the workshop Will approached me, notebook in hand.

"Hey, Nina, you look fantastic today. How about staying for a cup of coffee? Would you mind going over some of Hannah's notes? I don't think I got everything."

"Sure," I said, when my heart started beating again. "I'd like that."

A woman has a sixth sense about many situations, especially one that spells trouble for her. I was no exception.

I forgot about my happy, although routine, marriage to a wonderful man because Will was too attractive, too interesting, and far too available for me to have turned him down. It didn't happen the first time we had coffee together, or even the next few times we continued meeting after class. Will waited until I was jumping out of my skin for him before making his move.

I knew it was wrong, yet I couldn't help myself, or didn't want to. No one was holding a gun to my head; I was the one who should have declined his advances. He was a young, good-looking, single guy on the make, and I was married with children and had everything to lose. Why was I about to commit an act of adultery that would threaten my marriage if Ian ever found out? How could I explain it to our daughters? I tried to rationalize my actions by thinking my husband perhaps had lost interest in me, that he seemed distant during our dinner conversations, and that sex between us was infrequent. Unfortunately, it was all true.

"Nina, why don't we go back to my place for a decent cup of coffee," he said one day after class. Will might have wanted to brew a pot of decaf for me, but I knew it was an invitation to his bedroom. I followed him home in my car, repeating a mantra of how wrong this was, but I never turned back.

A daytime affair turned out to be easy to cover up. Shopping, lunch, movies, or theater matinees, and the two days at my job were some of the activities I pawned off as excuses to my husband, who had seemingly stopped caring where I'd been. Ian would typically ask me about my day as part of our dinner conversation, but I could tell by the distant look in his eyes that his mind was elsewhere. Maybe my straight-laced husband was having an affair of his own. Inconceivable and unthinkable, but wouldn't I have said the same about myself before meeting Will?

Will was always available in the afternoons because he worked the late shift at a twenty-four-hour big box store. Our trysts escalated from Tuesday after class to twice more during the week, as well as Saturday mornings when Ian was off on one of his field trips. We texted non-stop, and kept our illicit affair secret from Hannah's group. Some of the women, mesmerized by Will's tales, still met for coffee before our workshop began and we were generally late for class, which didn't go over well with our leader.

"Listen, folks," she'd said barging into our coffee salon. "I'm not going to hold up students who arrive on time to wait for you guys while you finish your lattes. It's not fair. We have two hours in the community room and if you want to give up fifteen or twenty minutes of that to gossip go right ahead, but we are starting on time and not staying late."

We obediently dumped our drinks and followed her to the private room set aside for our writing course.

Will was a natural-born writer and on those occasions when we weren't in bed, he'd show me manuscripts that he felt weren't appropriate for Hannah's class. The work was incredible, even with typos and incorrect grammar, and I encouraged him to finish at least some of the shorter pieces so they could be submitted to literary journals for publication. He agreed, but said he'd probably need an editor. Naturally, I offered my services but Will refused, mumbling something about not wanting to saddle me with extra work. I didn't think much about it at the time except how considerate I thought he was.

Our class had collectively decided to extend our initial eight-week course into ongoing sessions, and Hannah received approval for the open-ended schedule if we agreed to arrive on time. I didn't care about skipping the pre-class coffee klatch because I knew I had Will to myself afterwards.

At twenty dollars per student, per class, Hannah was making herself a nice little bundle, in cash. She must have been spending a good part of it at a new salon because her dull brown hair that a mouse would have sneered at had turned a golden blond color with even lighter blond high-lights commonly seen on red-carpet celebrities like Kate Hudson or her famous mom, Goldie Hawn. Someone had taught Hannah how to use makeup, and she'd probably hired a personal shopper because she'd begun to wear ex-pensive, fitted linen jackets over sexy lace camisoles and de-signer jeans. If Will noticed these improvements he kept it to himself because he never mentioned it to me, even when I cross-examined him.

"Why would I look at her when I have you?" he replied.

And I believed him.

Our secretive meetings went on for weeks although late-ly we spent more time dressed and talking about our writing projects rather than jumping into bed. The initial passion was beginning to wane, and I knew it was time to call it quits. The guilt was getting to me big time notwithstanding Ian's growing disinterest in my days. Or so I thought. I lost track of time one Tuesday afternoon in Will's apartment, and arrived home a little before five o'clock. I was surprised to find Ian already there.

"Where have you been?" he said, in a hostile voice.

"Well, hello to you too. I was out shopping," I said, moving in his direction to plant a kiss on his cheek. He pushed me away.

"I don't see any bags."

"No, I couldn't find what I wanted," I said, feeling my throat close up.

"I guess you found something or someone else you wanted. Don't bother to deny it. I took half a day off and was going to surprise you at the bookstore to take you out for coffee when I bumped into your teacher. She said you left early with a young man, like you do every Tuesday. What's going on, Nina? Who is he?" my husband said, this time with a slight tremor to his voice.

So Hannah had passive-aggressively let Ian know that I was seeing someone, and frankly, even though I felt my heart drop, it was a relief. I had worried that sooner or later word would get back to my fellow classmates and worse, to my husband as these things usually do. Naturally, I'd hoped to end the affair before Ian found out, but it was obviously too late for that.

"You were going to meet me for a date?" I said, incredulously. I couldn't remember the last time my husband had done anything near approaching a romantic gesture.

"Yes. I wanted to discuss something of importance with you, but that can wait," he said. "What the hell is going on with you?"

My husband of twenty years who'd been loyal, loving, and true had tears in his eyes as he waited for the answer he knew was coming.

"Ian, I won't deny it. There has been someone else. I've been unfaithful to you, and I don't want to make it worse by lying," I said, the tears beginning to flow. "I'm so sorry and ashamed."

"Is this what you want? Another man? A divorce?" he said, his voice still quavering. "Do you love him?"

"No! And I don't want a divorce. You're the only man I've ever loved. I don't know what made me do it. I never wanted to cheat on you. It just…happened."

"Nina, things like that don't just happen. Did he seduce you? Did he try to get you drunk?" Ian said, struggling to give me a way out.

"Stop. It was my fault. Yes, I was flattered by the attention of a younger man and more so because you and I seem to be growing apart. When I ask you what's wrong, you say 'business' and leave it at that. It's not an excuse, but we used to share everything; now it's like living with a stranger, and with the girls gone…I was lonely. I'm not saying this because I want you to take any of the blame, but maybe we had to come this far to start talking again," I said. I had to hope that my husband would find it in his heart to believe and forgive me, and give our marriage a second chance.

"I'm not letting you off the hook, but I'll admit that I'm guilty of not explaining what's going on in my life. That's what I wanted to talk to you about today. I've been putting it off for weeks. Our company is being taken over by a huge accounting firm, and some of us older guys will probably be replaced with kids right out of school. They'll give us a decent kiss-off package, but it'll be tough for me to find another position that comes close to the salary I'm making," he said, slumping into the sofa.

I sat next to him and took his hand. "Oh, how I wish you had told me that. I knew something was going on and I should have pushed the subject, but you clammed up whenever I did."

"Nina, I didn't want to worry you, or the girls."

"I worry more when you don't tell me what's on your mind," I said, breathing a sigh of relief that he hadn't tossed aside my hand.

"What matters now is that I want you to give up this guy and attend to our marriage," my husband said in the business-like tone he used for the most serious of topics. When our daughters graduated from high school he'd sat them down like members of the board and explained exactly what their responsibilities would be in college. They were straight-faced listening to their dad, who they loved and respected even if he treated them like employees, while making his point.

Ian's official plea almost sounded like I had to get back to work in the garden and water the lawn, but I was grateful that he wasn't asking for a divorce. Was this his way of saying he'd forgive me, even if it weren't right away?

"Ian, I am committed to our marriage and don't want out. I love you, not him. The affair is over as of now. I promise. Can we try to make this right?"

"Honey," Ian said, losing his formal voice, "I know I'm not the most exciting husband, and I've had a lot on my mind lately, but you have to know how much I love you and what you and the girls mean to me. I'd be lost without my family. Maybe I've been spending too much time away from you on the weekends with the camera group. It helped keep my mind off the business situation."

"But that's your favorite hobby. I don't want you to give it up. Maybe I need to find more activities to keep me busy. I guess the empty-nest syndrome hit harder than I expected. I'm going to see if I can work full-time to bring in more of a salary. We're in this together."

"I appreciate that, but financially we're okay for the moment and I think your time could be better spent concentrating on your writing. Maybe you should start by sending in a few articles to the local paper. You did that in college, remember? That's how we met. I needed to find out about the girl with the weird sense of humor."

"Weird?" I said, laughing through my tears. "You told me it was esoteric and sardonic."

"Yeah, that too," he said, and pulled me close. "We'll get through this, sweetheart."

My husband and I talked away the rest of the early evening, and went out to dinner to celebrate a new beginning. When we returned home, I made a big bowl of popcorn and we stayed up late to watch an old corny movie. Everything familiar about our intimacy rushed back to me as I looked at Ian with a new tenderness. I had learned a valuable lesson that I wouldn't soon forget.

Ian hadn't questioned me about the young man Hannah told him I'd left with, and there was no need to explain anything further. I'd hurt him enough. Now it was time to continue mending the rift in my marriage. I felt a moral obligation to drop out of the class, and decided to stop by The Book Café on Tuesday to tell Hannah in person that I wouldn't be able to attend any more sessions, and I'd catch up with Will to confirm that our affair was over.

Hannah was an excellent teacher and my writing had improved tremendously in the weeks I'd taken her course. Ian was right. I was going to focus on my craft and send in some articles to *The Bugle*, our local paper, and then I'd try my hand at fiction. I'd keep my two-day-a-week job until Ian found out more about our financial future.

The following Tuesday I arrived at the bookstore a little early hoping to catch Will before the class began. I hadn't answered his texts, so perhaps he'd gotten the unspoken message, but I still had to make it clear to him that we wouldn't continue seeing each other. I would tell Hannah that I was going to be working full-time, a harmless white lie, and wouldn't be able to manage coming in anymore.

When I entered the bookstore that day Will was already there, speaking with Hannah. Her hand was on his arm, and his eyes were on her breasts. In a split second I realized what was going on. Will was carrying on with Hannah, and probably had been while cheating with me. They both began to laugh at something Will said while Hannah's hand crept further up his arm stopping to fondle his tattoos along the way. They didn't see me, and I decided not to interfere with their rendezvous. I sent Will a text that we were officially over, and an email to Hannah explaining that I was dropping out of her workshop because I needed more time to devote to a new endeavor.

My breakout novel, *The Housewife's Revenge,* somehow became an instant bestseller. Ian received an unexpected generous package when he was let go and became my full-time manager, arranging local signings in the beginning of my new career, and going on to planning full-scale book tours. I had to quit my job at the publishing house because I became one of their hottest clients. My second book, *Be Very Afraid,* is about to hit the stands and they predict another blockbuster.

Hannah Fox no longer conducts classes at the bookstore. It seems that according to store policy she was not supposed to be charging us, and one of her students, who'd made little progress with her writing, demanded her money back from the store manager, who'd been unaware of Hannah's monetary practices. Will Viner sent me a text several weeks after my first novel was published asking if my offer to edit his work was still standing. I told him it wasn't, and that was the last I heard from him.

Even though Hannah probably had no clue that I'd been involved with Will, I have to admit that I was a little bit happy when I heard she'd been fired. She'd find a job elsewhere, and if she wanted to continue seeing Will, that was her business. Thinking about a suitable payback for Will, who was cheating on me while I was cheating on Ian, was just plain ridiculous. The Bible teaches us not to take revenge, but according to my editor, it would help sell books.

Ian and I have never been happier. We had a few rough patches to muddle through, but he and I were committed to making progress with our relationship. Ian alternates weekends between his photography group and making plans with me, plus we enjoy our two or three date nights a week. When Polly and Piper are home for an occasional weekend, we ignore their eye-rolling when they see Ian kissing me, but I can tell they're pleased to have parents who are still very much in love with each other.

Through counseling and prayer Ian was able to fully forgive me for breaking our vows, and we managed to elevate our marriage to a new level filled with love, understanding, and mutual respect.

Like most fairytales, we plan to live happily ever after.

A CHANGE OF PLANTS

Lara opened the kitchen window to view what should have been a perfect setting on a cool south Florida day in January. Several flowering shrubs surrounded a fruit-laden guava tree adorned with three orchid plants hanging from the trunk's thick, gnarled, pale limbs. Only this trio of limp, white-spotted, and pathetic-looking orchids entwined around wooden planters spoiled the scenery. She'd have to learn how to care for the orchids and bring them back to life, now that she had a new one. Perhaps someone in the apartment complex where she lived could give her advice. She'd noticed that residents left cards push-pinned to a cork board in the office with requests for baby sitters, dog walkers, and the like. Lara would post a flyer asking for help with the orchids.

I won't let them die. I can't allow that to happen. If I survived, so will they.

Lara had recently moved into the modest, ground-floor rental apartment at Garden Lakes in Boca Raton, a far cry from the luxurious mansion she'd left behind in the elegant town of Palm Beach, along with her abusive husband, Warren Spiker. It had been three months since Lara had been living on her own, and she was still plagued with nightmares of the frightening times she'd gone through with Warren. She tried to focus on finding a job because as much as she hadn't wanted to accept any financial offering from her husband before the forthcoming divorce decree, she was forced to do so to pay rent and other bills. Warren didn't show up at the settlement meeting, but his family's attorney took care of all the details. Her in-laws, Sarah and Hugh Spiker, were there to support their daughter-in-law. They'd learned about the son who'd emotionally and physically abused Lara for almost the entire year of their marriage.

What a difference from the charming Romeo she'd first met at a church dance. She'd fallen hard for Warren Spiker and, against her parents' wishes, married him six weeks later.

Lara's best friend, Iris Avery, who worked as the property manager at Garden Lakes, had helped her find an apartment after the separation from Warren. Iris thought moving away from Palm Beach and the terrible memories there would be wise. Lara agreed. She had also reconciled with her family, who lived in the nearby town of Boynton Beach, and was happy they would finally be able to spend time together.

Long before Lara separated from Warren, Iris had noticed bruises on her friend's arms not even a few weeks after the wedding.

"Is everything alright at home?" she said.

"Oh yes, I'm still unpacking and settling in if you can believe it."

"I'm a little concerned about those marks on your upper arms. How did that happen?" Iris asked, with a discerning eye.

"You know, with carrying stuff around that big house I keep knocking into things. I should be more careful," Lara said.

"You'd tell me if things weren't right between you and Warren, wouldn't you? I know he has a temper. It was pretty scary at the rehearsal dinner, and the wedding reception."

"My husband is a perfectionist, so he tends to fly off the handle about little things, but then he forgets about it. Really, Iris, you don't have to worry."

"Lara, he called you a major pain in the ass in front of everyone at the rehearsal dinner. That's not exactly a little thing," Iris said, remembering back to that evening when Warren embarrassed his bride-to-be.

"Please let it go. The wine he ordered wasn't available and he didn't like the one they substituted," Lara said, trying to erase the unpleasant memory from her mind and ease Iris's concern.

"I care about you. You can always come stay with us if need be."

"Yeah, right. You and Milt and your three kids and your two dogs. That's all you need is one more in the house. I'll be fine."

Maybe she should have listened to her friend before Warren's conduct became intolerable, but Lara was a firm believer in her marriage vows. She felt sure her husband would settle down after those first months following the wedding and honeymoon, each disastrous by all accounts. Her parents refused to attend the wedding or pay for any part of it, which started things off on the wrong foot. Her father warned her not to marry him because both he and his wife had noticed something in Warren's nature that was off-putting, and they told her if she continued her relationship with him, there'd be very little communication between the families.

Warren's parents, who owned a chain of furniture stores throughout south Florida, were wealthy and insisted on paying for not only the lavish wedding, but also the ten-day honeymoon at an exclusive resort on the island of Antigua. Lara had protested that they were doing too much for them, but Warren told her in no uncertain terms to keep her mouth shut and let him handle his family since hers wasn't doing their share. Lara quickly learned to retreat when Warren was in a bad mood, and didn't further the discussion.

The wedding ceremony went according to plan with Iris standing up for her, and Warren's younger brother, Ted, as the best man. Warren's father was kind enough to walk her down the aisle before joining his wife in the front pew of the church. The reception at The Breakers Hotel was a different story. Warren punched Ted to the floor for dancing too close to Lara, and even though his bride tried to explain that it was innocent, Ted left the party feeling hurt and humiliated. The Spikers saw the incident, but wanting to keep the peace said nothing to their older son. They reasoned that perhaps the boys had had a bit too much to drink. Shortly after the altercation, which most of the guests had witnessed, the invitees started to trickle out saying it was getting late, or gave other last-minute excuses to distance themselves from the distasteful event.

Warren's anger didn't end when the reception did. That night in their honeymoon suite he berated Lara for her part in what he called "a smarmy affair" with Ted, and they went to sleep without making love. Her new husband had calmed down by morning and ordered breakfast to be sent to the room. As he poured coffee into a fine bone china cup for her with just the right amount of milk and the sweetener he knew she preferred, he apologized, blaming his outburst on pre-wedding stress. Lara accepted his apology wanting to begin their life together with love-making, and not arguments, but her hand trembled slightly as she lifted the cup to her lips.

When they checked into the Ocean View Resort in Antigua, Warren raised boisterous objections to their room size and location, and in order to placate him, the front desk executive upgraded the couple from the bridal to the presidential suite. Luckily, the hotel had a last-minute cancelation and wanting to avoid further discord with Warren, the manager accommodated him with the larger suite. The senior Spikers were regular clients, and often traveled with friends who stayed there also. The manager didn't want word to get back to them that their son's honeymoon hadn't gone perfectly.

After they were settled and unpacked, Lara changed into her bathing suit.

"You're not wearing that…that piece of cloth to the beach," he blurted out.

"It's a bikini…I thought you'd like it," Lara said, her stomach muscles tensing.

"I don't want my wife parading around a fancy resort looking like some cheap hooker. Save it for our backyard pool, which is more than you ever had growing up. Don't forget who paid for the Palm Beach estate we're going to live in while your parents sit around on their fat asses in one of those adult sleep-away camp communities in Boynton Beach. They did nothing for their only daughter. Get out of that suit and put something decent on."

Lara felt a hitch in her breathing as she complied with her husband's request.

Things got progressively worse between the two, and several weeks after they returned from their honeymoon he smacked her over a silly piece of nonsense. She was to have set the table with the linen napkins he'd left on the buffet, but Lara thought the blue and white striped ones looked more summery. It would be the first time he hit her, but certainly not the last. He was jealous of every man she came in contact with including the gardener, the pool service contractor, and even the kid who delivered the newspaper. Lara was frequently black and blue, and had to wear loose-fitting trousers with long-sleeved shirts to cover up the bruises. She never left the house without her oversized black sunglasses, and took to wrapping a scarf around her neck. There would always be an apology at the end of the day, usually accompanied by flowers, or her favorite chocolates, and she foolishly accepted his pleas for forgiveness and a promise never to strike her again. Several weeks of Warren being sweet and loving would follow until another imagined offense cropped up, and he would take out his anger on his wife, emotionally and physically.

Iris was the first person to realize something was wrong, but Lara would never admit to saying more than she'd been clumsy taking the laundry upstairs, or had gotten scratched and bruised by working in the garden. She and Warren were fine.

Lara's mother-in-law also suspected what was going on and invited her out to lunch. The young couple had recently celebrated their first anniversary and Lara chose to wear the diamond-flower earrings Warren had given her. When he'd asked what she'd like for their anniversary, she mentioned she'd always longed for diamond studs—nothing too big—but that could be worn every day.

"That's awfully pedestrian, but what did I expect from someone who was raised by hillbillies. I'll find something better," he'd said, and the conversation was closed. Warren never missed a chance to denigrate her parents, and Lara knew it was hopeless to try and defend them.

Sarah was already seated at a table in Palm Beach's legendary Ta-Boo Restaurant on Worth Avenue when her daughter-in-law approached. Lara wore a lightweight maxidress with one of her signature scarves that covered up the black and blue marks, but even with makeup and dark glasses, Sarah became aware of the injuries.

"He's beating you, isn't he," she'd said to Lara after they ordered their entrees. "Don't bother to deny it."

"I swear it's not my fault."

"Oh, my dear, I never would think that. It's time you and I had a talk, but first I'm ordering two glasses of wine for us," Sarah said, and signaled the server. A minute later he brought over two goblets of Sauvignon Blanc.

"Wine at lunch?" Lara said, trying to ease the moment.

Sarah ignored the rhetorical question and continued with her explanation of Warren's background.

"You see, Hugh and I have known about Warren's temper for years. Even as a little boy, he'd bang on his brother's head if we were out of the room, and we could never keep a nanny or even a baby sitter because of his behavior. When Warren was ten, we found a compassionate therapist, a Doctor Tanner, who was enormously helpful. He started him on a prescription for bipolar disorder and Warren's whole demeanor changed. He became calmer and more outgoing, and we thought he was 'cured.' Hugh and I wanted it so badly for him that we ignored the signs that his old behavior was resurfacing a short while before your wedding. Warren must have stopped the medication after he met you, thinking he didn't need it anymore, but bipolar doesn't work that way. I also found out that he'd left Dr. Tanner's care. Hugh urged Warren to follow up with him or even with another doctor, but our son told us he realized how difficult he'd been in the past, and was determined to change for the better," Sarah said.

"He was wonderful when we first met. We still love each other. I don't know much about bipolar, but maybe he'd go back on his meds if I mention it to him," Lara said, happy to have a glass of wine to calm her nerves. "We need to get back where we were."

"Not every person with bipolar disorder becomes violent, but it could be causing that in Warren's case. I think things have gone too far for you to involve yourself, even if you are his wife. When Warren first introduced you to us we were thrilled and knew you'd be a wonderful influence on him. Warren was already twenty-five at that point, and we felt he was capable of making the right decisions about his mental health. Obviously, we were wrong," Sarah said.

"I don't know what gets into him, or why he becomes so enraged if I even greet a neighbor. Most of the time we get along great and have so much fun together, and he can be just the sweetest husband ever. Did you see the earrings he gave me for our anniversary?" Lara said, and pulled the scarf away from around her neck before realizing that she was now giving Sarah full view of the marks she'd suffered from their last row.

"Oh, my god. He did that to you. You've got to get out of the house. I'm afraid for you. Hugh and I can make arrangements for a legal separation and a place to stay, but right now I'm concerned for your safety. It's the only way if he's not on his medication, and we'll do our best to try to make that happen, but there are no guarantees that he'll listen to us. Perhaps if he gets himself straightened out, the two of you can try again, but I can't stand by and let this go on because it'll only get worse. I never should have waited this long to say something," Sarah said, horrified at her daughter-in-law's condition, and she'd only seen the neck injuries.

"Sarah, I love my husband and we need to figure it out together. You and Hugh have been wonderful to me, and have made up for my parents more or less abandoning me. I promise to talk it out with Warren tonight and ask him to go to counseling with me. I'm sure he'll agree. He tells me all the time how much he adores me and that he couldn't live without me. He won't risk the idea of divorce. All couples need to work through their first year together," Lara said. "I'm not giving up on my marriage."

"I agree, but that does not and should never involve physical abuse. Hugh and I are going to step in if we see that he continues to mistreat you. I wish you had called us, or the police."

"Sarah, I can't call the police on my husband. Maybe he's just stressed out from the office."

"Lara, Hugh took his sons into the business after they graduated from college. Ted has worked out so well that Hugh is sure he'll be able to take over the company when he retires. He wanted the same for Warren. That's our legacy for the boys. The truth is that Warren does very little in the office. Hugh can't let him deal with clients, so he keeps him busy with paper work, ordering supplies, or phantom projects that will never go anywhere."

"But his title…" Lara said, sounding confused because Warren was constantly bragging about his stature in the company, and the changes he was going to make as soon as he took it over one day.

"That's all for show. Luckily, the business is thriving and we can continue to cover his expenses and his mistakes. He's our son and we love him also, but no one should have to live under these conditions. The earrings are lovely, but I'm sure they're not the ones you wanted because Warren mentioned your idea of studs to me. I brought these along for you, from Hugh and me," Sarah said.

Lara opened the blue velvet box and saw the brilliant diamond studs twinkling up at her. They were exactly the size and setting she'd dreamed about.

"They're beautiful. Thank you so much. I'll call Hugh later to thank him," Lara said.

The two women finished their lunch and changed the gloomy conversation by discussing the latest movies they'd seen, and book recommendations. Lara tucked the little jewelry box inside her handbag, and kissed Sarah goodbye, thanking her again for the gift and lunch. Sarah made her promise to keep her advised if anything further happened. On the drive home, Lara promised herself that their marriage would have a new beginning.

Sarah must have been exaggerating about Warren's participation in the business. Hugh probably isn't giving his son enough encouragement to do a better job. I'm not going to mention that situation tonight because if it's true, I don't want Warren to be embarrassed. I'm sure he pulls his weight at the office or they wouldn't have made him the Vice President.

Before Warren arrived home that evening, Lara set the table with the linens he'd left out on the buffet in the morning. She reapplied her makeup to cover up some of the remaining bruises. Although they had faded, she still wore a chiffon scarf loosely knotted toward the back of her neck so that the silky, white train tumbled halfway down her back. She changed into leggings and a pink sweater with a deep v-neck, and was satisfied with the result: a little sexy, but not tacky. Lara pulled her dark, shiny hair into a high ponytail, which highlighted the diamond flower earrings he'd given to her.

She'd made a special anniversary dinner and was about to open a bottle of white wine when she heard Warren's key in the door. He kissed her hello and complimented the way the earrings looked.

"Excellent choice of wine," he said, even though he had suggested it before he left that morning. "I could use a glass about now after the day I had."

"Busy in the office, darling?" she asked, ready to play along with him.

"Yeah, a few new clients that Ted couldn't handle so big brother here had to save his skin, again," he said.

"I'm sure he's glad you're there to help," Lara said.

"Are you kidding? He's dead meat without me holding his hand. Of course, I let him take the credit so Dad doesn't fire him. I suppose I'll have to keep him on after Dad retires," Warren said. "That's the right thing to do."

Lara didn't know what to believe. This was totally contrary to what Sarah had confided in her. She sipped her wine in silence for a moment, and fixed a plate for Warren.

They sat down to a lovely meal and began to chat away amiably with Lara channeling the discussion in his direction, relieved that the office-talk had come to an end. The evening was going well. Sarah wouldn't have to worry. They'd get their marriage on track and Lara would continue to hold fast to her vows. There was time to talk about seeing a therapist.

"Babe, did you drop off my cleaning like I asked you to?" he said.

"Absolutely, on my way to meet your mother for lunch," Lara said. "Your suit will be ready tomorrow. I'll pick it up in the afternoon."

"How'd lunch go?"

"Fine. I'm so fortunate to have them as in-laws."

"Yeah, they're super fine," Warren said, with a note of sarcasm to his voice. "Oh, where's the ticket for the dry cleaners. I have to pass by there tomorrow, so I'll save you a trip."

"It's in my purse. I'll get it," she said, beginning to rise from her chair.

"Nah, you sit. You worked hard enough getting this meal out, which is delicious. All my favorites. And don't you dare clear the table tonight. You get the night off, at least until we get into the bedroom," he said, and leaned down to kiss her cheek.

"Honey, that's really sweet of you and after you worked so hard today," she said, not knowing if it was the truth or not.

"No biggie. So, where's your bag? In the bedroom?"

"Yes, on the chaise. It should be in my wallet."

Lara relaxed back in her seat and poured another half glass of wine. Tonight was making up for the troubling times she'd endured over the past several months, and she would do her part to ensure their marriage continued on an even keel. So what if he picked out the linens and the wine? Warren's participation in the office probably fell somewhere in between what Sarah had told her, and his own interpretation. Although Hugh was certainly pleasant in social settings and had always been kind to her, both Warren and Ted had called him a fierce taskmaster at work.

Since Warren didn't want her to find a job, maybe she wasn't spending enough time taking care of the house. Although they had a weekly housekeeper for the heavy cleaning, she could take on other projects in the house like organizing their closets or rearranging the pantry. Now with Warren offering to clear the table and pick up the dry cleaning, chores he rarely did, perhaps her husband realized that he'd been overly harsh with her. The two of them would work together to build their relationship.

Oh no, the jewelry box! I left it in my purse. I wanted to explain about that before he saw the studs. Maybe he won't notice because I tucked it away in one of the side pockets.

The next instant Warren came running down the stairs with her bag in one hand, and the little velvet box in the other.

"What the hell is this?" he said, his face bright red.

Lara tried to make light of the situation. "Oh, I meant to tell you. Your parents gave me an anniversary present."

"I already gave you diamond earrings. Why on earth do you need another pair, and what right do my parents have giving you anything more?" he said, slamming her bag down on the granite floor. "You know what I think of these precious little studs you wanted so badly? Do you? This is what I think of them," he said, and threw the box across the room shattering an exquisite hand-painted porcelain vase that had been a wedding present. It was a designer piece, and a gift from the artist herself. Now it was irretrievably broken.

"Those earrings are going back in the morning."

"I was going to show them to you, but we got caught up with having such a nice dinner and the wine…" she started to say, placing her hands on the table to quell their shaking.

"Shut up. Do you think I'm an idiot?" he said, approaching her with a menacing look in his eyes.

Instinctively, Lara knew a beating would be forthcoming if she didn't stop it by any means possible. Her only defense would be to go on the offensive. Inhaling deeply, she took the chance and stood up to be face to face with him.

"Frankly, I do think you're an idiot. You've ruined our anniversary, and our marriage. I could have called the police on you any number of times, but I hoped against all possible hope that you would change. Your mother filled me in on your childhood behavior, and the therapy you walked away from. Here's the biggest surprise: your own mother advised me to file for a separation, but I told her that I loved you and wanted to make our marriage work. Well, it can't. I want a divorce."

Warren stood there shell-shocked at his wife's diatribe and finally spoke.

"Maybe I have been a little tough on you, but you're the same pain in the ass you were the day I married you. You think I can't get a woman ten times better than you?" he said, practically sneering at her.

"I'm sure you can. Here, you can give her these earrings," she said, removing them from her ears and plunking them down on the table. She walked over to where the broken vase had fallen and picked up the box with the diamond studs that Sarah had given her.

"I'm going to Ted's. We'll talk about this in the morning," Warren said, and slammed the front door behind him as he left.

"Make sure you remind him about how much you help out in the office," she said, shouting after Warren even though there was no way he could have heard her through the solid oak double doors.

As soon as Lara knew her husband had driven off, she made three phone calls. The first was devastating because she had to admit to Sarah that she wanted to go through with the separation and could use her help with the process. The second call was to her parents. Her mother answered on the first ring and after apologies and a few tears from both sides, Lara told her about the plans she was about to make. Then, she called Iris, who was only too happy to hear from her friend. She promised to help her relocate to Boca Raton.

After breakfast, Lara typed up a note asking for help with her orchids:

Please contact me if you can show me how to take care of the orchids in my backyard. They're in very bad shape! I'm in apartment #1646, or call my cell phone: 561-555-2785. Thank you. Lara

She walked over to the office and after pinning her card to the corkboard, stopped in to see Iris.

"Hey girl, how's it going? You all settled in?" Iris asked.

"Just about. I'm going to run over to the market. You need anything?"

"Would you mind picking up a sandwich for me? We're so busy and shorthanded I know I won't have a chance to get out for lunch," Iris said, "and I have a couple of appointments scheduled for new renters. This place is hot. I guess it's because the location is so convenient. Have your folks been over yet?"

"A couple of times, when they're not socializing with their buddies up in one of the gated communities. I never remember which one," Lara said, kidding around.

"Ah yes, the adult sleep-away camps in Boynton Beach. Valencias, Venetians, Villa this and that. They're probably having the time of their lives," Iris said.

Lara bristled slightly at the mention of adult camps because Warren had been so condescending when he used the same term. But, the truth was that her folks were enjoying the carefree lifestyle in their community and had made some wonderful new friends.

"Yep, they do love it, and it's only fifteen minutes from me so we're making up for lost time. Where's Michelle?" Lara said. "And there's hardly any coffee pods."

"I'm short staffed because Michelle is only going to be

working here part time. She's training to become a massage therapist, not that Boca doesn't have enough of those. She'll only be here twice a week. I'll have to hire someone soon because I can't run the office and keep up with the coffee supplies and be out showing apartments to prospective clients."

"I'll pick up some pods until you have time to place an order, but what about Nancy or Sue? Can't they pitch in?" Lara said, filling the coffee maker with fresh water and setting out what was left of the different flavored pods. Memories of happier times with Warren relaxing in their favorite local coffee shop flooded back to her, but she quickly put those thoughts out of her mind.

"Not usually, because Nancy has her hands full keeping up in the accounting department, and Sue's the landscape liaison. I'll put something online about the job. That's how I started here, and it was kind of fun driving that big old golf cart around the property showing our model apartments. Then the corporate office bumped me up to manager when Mary left to have a baby," Iris said.

"I'd be happy to pick up a sandwich for you, but do you think I could handle that job?" Lara said. "I haven't worked since before I met Warren. I want to start paying my own way."

"Of course you could handle it. I didn't even think to ask you. That'd be perfect. Michelle's due back in about a half hour. Can you get here by then because I'd like to ask her to show you around and explain the procedures, especially the security we have in place. Setting up the reception area is part of the job too, but it's only coffee and a few cookies. It's important to make a friendly impression, although I won't have to worry about that with you. What do you say? Just think, you could walk to work, and you'll get a break in the rent," Iris said.

"I would love to give it a shot. My mother-in-law is so

generous, and now my folks have been helping out, but I need to be on my own," Lara said.

"Let's do it. You'll have to fill out an application for the corporate office, but that's just a rubber stamp. You're hired. We have a staff meeting Tuesdays at six. You'll have a chance to get to know everyone and the workings of the place, and usually there's a bottle of wine after we finish up. Now, please, before I pass out, turkey on rye with mustard," Iris said.

A week later Lara began her new job as a leasing assistant and kept busy all day showing prospective renters the different apartments that were available, as well as the beautiful community pool area and well-equipped gym. When she had a break, she'd straighten up the lounge area in the reception room, making sure there were enough coffee pods and cookies for residents or anyone else who stopped by to find out about the community. Lara enjoyed interacting with people and although some of the men were friendly enough, she had no desire to start dating and discouraged any would-be suitors.

I wonder if my husband would be proud of me, living on my own with a new job. Oh, Warren, why couldn't our marriage have worked out!

Lara began to make friends with a few of the girls she'd met in the gym. They had invited her to join their monthly book club, which she was glad to accept. It was something Warren never allowed her to do.

"How do I know what kind of people you'll be with or what type of trash they read?" he'd said. The point was too ridiculous to argue, and at the time she was still healing from his last thrashing and couldn't take the chance of another by going against his wishes.

After a month of living in the apartment, Lara finally began to dress in sleeveless tank tops and cotton skirts or long shorts, much more accommodating to the warm weather than the layers of clothing she'd previously worn to camouflage her injuries.

Sue happened to see Lara's note about her ailing orchids and mentioned the man who owned the landscaping company that serviced Garden Lakes.

"Trey and I meet once a week to go over the property to make sure everything is taken care of, which it usually is. He's super nice and if I weren't married...oh, he'd be just my type," Sue said. "You'll like him, and he's noticed you. He wanted to know all about the pretty girl with the long ponytail who was driving around in the golf cart."

"I'm sure he's fine, but I'm not interested in dating, just getting my orchids in shape," Lara said.

"Sometimes he stops in at the staff meetings, so I can introduce the two of you then," Sue said, with an obvious wink. "You can't say no to that."

"I'll be happy to meet him, but forget about getting us together for anything other than gardening."

Warren had recently begun to email her pleading for another chance, saying that he was back on his medication and seeing Dr. Tanner twice a week. He swore he still loved her and wanted to make up for the year of hell he'd put her through. They weren't officially divorced yet, and he wanted to prove he was the man she'd first met. She found it difficult to ignore his emails and finally relented when he asked if they could speak on the phone.

"Please, Lara, we're still young. We can try again. If you don't want to live in Palm Beach, I'll come to Boca or we can even get a place in Boynton, near your folks. I'm doing much better at work now, and it'd be an easy commute. Dad's actually giving me real projects to handle now. You can even call him or Mom to check," he said, with a laugh. "I'm glad you didn't change your cell number. Can I take that as a sign that you'll still take my calls from now on?"

"Let's see how it goes," she said, trying to remain non-committal. Warren had seemed so sincere in his emails, and now he sounded genuinely interested in her welfare, and a reconciliation. Had she subconsciously been waiting for this day? Could she forgive his past injustices that almost broke her body and spirit?

"How about it? Let me come by and at least take you to dinner," he said.

"You mean a date night?" Lara said, not suppressing a smile. Warren sounded like the young man she first met at the church dance. Sweet, considerate, and loving. No wonder she'd married him so quickly.

"Call it whatever you like, but let's do it. How about this Saturday? Uh, unless you're busy," he said.

"No, I'm not and I'm not seeing anyone if that's what you mean. Saturday is fine. Should we meet at a restaurant? I can make a reservation," she said, having reservations of her own about their plans.

Maybe he deserves a second chance. It was terribly wrong of him to have abused me, but if his bipolar disorder was causing the change in his personality, then perhaps we can work it out now that he's back on his meds and seeing Dr. Tanner. As much as I've tried to forget him, he still holds a place in my heart. It's got to be worth a try because we did have some amazing times together, and I won't have to worry about anything if we're sitting in a restaurant. I could check out his story with his folks, but it's not right to involve them. I'm responsible for all my decisions now and I like it this way!

"Lara? You there?" he said.

"Oh sorry, I was just grabbing my coffee," she said, not wanting to share her private thoughts. "So, where shall we meet? Italian?"

"Don't worry about the details. I want to show you what a gentleman I am. I'll pick you up at seven and I'll take care of the restaurant," he said. "Someplace nice. I have your address. Any problem getting into the complex?"

"No, not really. Just dial my extension at the call box, and I'll buzz you through the gate. I'm in apartment 1646, on the ground floor," she said. "It's really a lovely place. I'm happy here."

"I'm glad. You should only have good things in your life from now on. We'll talk about that on Saturday," he said.

Her cell rang again as soon as she hung up with Warren. She didn't recognize the number, but it was local and the caller I.D. read Trey Field, the landscaper she'd briefly met when he stopped in at a staff meeting. He was as cute as Sue had predicted, but Lara was definitely not ready for any new relationships. She was nervous enough about the date she'd just made with Warren.

"Hello," she said.

"Lara? Hi, it's Trey. We met at the staff meeting."

He hardly needs to remind me. Who could forget those gorgeous golden-brown eyes with lashes he probably doesn't appreciate.

"Sure, hi Trey."

"We didn't have much time to talk about your orchids, but since I work in the community I'd be happy to help you out. I figured I better call first in case you see someone puttering around your backyard. If you like, I can stop by over the weekend and take a look at those plants. I'm pretty good with that stuff," Trey said.

"Thank you, but I don't want to disturb you on your weekend."

"No problem. I live nearby and I actually help out quite a few of your neighbors. I'll probably be there late in the day on Saturday," he said.

"That'd be great because they've gotten worse and I don't want to lose them. And even if I bought new orchids, they might not make it either. I don't have much of a green thumb, but I'm willing to learn. I work Saturdays, but I'm usually home by four, if that's convenient."

"Sure. Hope you like your job here," Trey said. "I've seen you buzzing around in the golf cart. Iris told me she hired her friend to work here."

"Yes, we go way back. I'm just getting back into the work force," she said, not wanting to go into further detail.

"You don't have to be home, so I won't bother you. I'll walk around back and check them out. Then I'll give you a call and we can see what's going on with those plants."

"Thanks, Trey. I'll be going out Saturday evening, but any time before six-thirty would be fine. I've got to save those plants," she said, more seriously than planned.

"And save them we will!"

Lara grabbed a quick bite before she walked over to the office. She had clients coming in for a second look-see, and they'd specifically asked for her even though Michelle was still on duty. They were scheduled for a showing at three, but Lara decided to arrive early to ask Iris about Trey.

"Hey, Iris. You busy?" Lara said.

"Always, and you have a client coming in soon. If you can get them to rent that townhouse they're interested in, you'll get a bonus. So, what's up?"

Lara decided not to mention her upcoming date with Warren to her friend because that had been such a sore subject in the past.

"You know Trey Field, right?"

"Sure, everyone knows him. You met him at the staff meeting. He owns the landscaping company that takes care of all the Garden Lakes properties. Nice guy. Cute, too. Don't tell me he asked you out? Didn't think you were up to dating yet, but you know, wouldn't be a bad idea," she said.

"Iris, I'd love to know how that brain of yours works because no one gets to the point quicker than you. No, I'm not dating him or anyone else. He called because he saw my note about the orchids. He offered to help me with them," Lara said.

"Our deal with his company is that they take care of all the lawns, trees and shrubbery, but residents are responsible for anything else that's planted, potted, or hanging from a tree…like your orchids. Why don't you dump those things—they're a mess," Iris said. "But on second thought, let Trey take a look at them. Maybe you should get to know him a little better."

"Iris, I want to save the orchids, not be in a romance novel. If Trey tells me they're diseased or whatever, I'll get rid of them, but if he thinks they have a chance, I'll take it."

"Oh, I see. So the orchids are a metaphor for your new life."

"Something like that. Hate to run, but I just saw my clients drive up. See you later," Lara said, and left to greet the family who would hopefully want to rent the townhouse.

Lara kept busy for the rest of the week taking care of the reception area when it was slow, and inspecting the model apartments to make sure the cleaning staff was doing their job. The people she'd shown the townhouse to signed a one-year lease, and Lara received a two-hundred dollar bonus.

She had a couple of appointments on Saturday morning,

but left the office at four to clean up, and perhaps meet with Trey. There was no sign of his truck, so she went about her business until it was time to change into something pretty for her date with Warren.

I can't believe I'm actually looking forward to seeing him. Maybe there is hope for us. The first step would be counseling if we wanted to try again. I'm sure he'd understand that.

At six-thirty, her bell rang and she assumed it was Trey. She had gotten ready early just in case he showed up, and opened the door to meet the landscaper. It was Warren.

"Hello Lara," he said, handing her a bouquet of flowers. "You look beautiful."

"Warren, I wasn't expecting you so soon. How'd you get in?"

"I was hoping for a kiss or a hug hello," he said good-naturedly. "Someone pulled in ahead of me, and I guess I kind of sneaked through the gate before it closed. Is that a no-no?"

"Actually, it is. There's a sign saying one car at a time," she said, taking the flowers.

"I must have missed it. Sorry, I'll do better next time," he said, with the same boyish grin that had won her over at their first meeting. "May I come in?"

"Of course. Thank you for the flowers. I'll put them in some water. Come on in and have a seat. Be right with you," she said.

"The place looks fantastic, but you always had a nice touch with decorating," Warren said.

Strange that he would say that after he chose every chair, table, and sofa for our house. But he's trying. And that smile...

"Thank you," she called out from the kitchen. "It's comfortable."

While she was filling the vase, Warren joined her in the kitchen.

"Wow, pretty spacious for a rental," he said.

"Yes, all the apartments have good layouts." She paused before adding, "I'm working here now."

"Working? Doing what?" he said, trying to keep the cynicism out of his voice.

"I show people the model apartments they may want to rent. And I take care of the reception area," she said, hoping to sound sure of herself. "I'm thinking about going back to school to become a real estate broker."

"You take care of it? What are you, a maid?" he said, ignoring her remark about developing a new career. Realizing he'd gone overboard with sarcasm he added, "You always were a neatnik. I'm sure they're happy to have you on board."

"Everyone is super nice, and Iris treats me well," she said, ignoring his questions that bordered on insults.

He's nervous. I can't pick on him for every little thing. He'll have to get used to me working if he wants to get back together. I'm not going to sit around all day and do nothing.

"Oh, Iris. That's right. She's the big deal here," he said, looking out the window. "Hold it! Who's in your backyard? What's he doing here? Who is that?"

Lara became alarmed at his tone, and began to explain that it was probably the landscaper who was going to have a look at her dying orchids. Warren grabbed her by the arm, his hand digging sharply into her shoulder and pulled her away from the open window.

"What are you doing? You're hurting me," she said, wincing in pain. "What's wrong with you! I thought you were supposed to be on your meds so you wouldn't act like this, but obviously that hasn't happened. Let go of me!"

"Same old stupid girl...trying to make me jealous. You haven't changed either! You knew I'd be here, so you decided to show me up by having another man stop by. What kind of crap is that? I don't believe you for a minute. Who is it?" he said, and slapped the side of her face.

She screamed and while struggling to get out of his grip, the front door swung open.

"Hello? Everything okay in here? Your door wasn't locked and I thought I heard someone yell out. See a mouse or something?" said Trey, walking into the kitchen and keeping his cool while sizing up the situation. "Lara, any problems? Do you need me to call for security?"

"No. That won't be necessary. Warren was just leaving," she said, not bothering to introduce the two men.

"You bet I am," he said. "I never should have married you in the first place."

"Okay, buddy, time to go," Trey said, taking Warren by the arm and roughly guiding him out to his car.

"Let go of me, you dirt-digger," Warren said.

"You have exactly two minutes to leave this complex or I'll contact security, and they have no problem calling the sheriff's department on jerks like you," Trey said, as he opened the car door and shoved Warren into the driver's seat. "Don't come back."

Lara was sitting on the sofa holding back tears when Trey knocked on the open door.

"It's me again. Okay to come in?" he asked.

"Sure, and thank you," she said, trying to present a calm façade.

"He didn't hurt you, did he? That was quite a scream." Trey said.

"It was more of a shock than anything. That was my ex-husband, or at least he will be when the divorce is final," she said, not wanting to go into Warren's history of abusive behavior. That part of her life had ended for good with Warren's departure.

"You know, it looks like you were all dressed up to go out. I guess it must be about dinner time. I got a little lost in those orchid plants of yours. Come on, let me take you out for some food, and speaking of food, have you been feeding the orchids?" he said.

"I didn't know they were hungry," she said, finally able to smile.

"We'll discuss all that over dinner. They're not in the greatest shape, but with a little care I think we can fix them up. That guava is a beauty, and I like the way the planters look on it. Like they belong," Trey said.

"I know the feeling."

"Then let's try to bring them back to life. I'll cart over a few new ones from the nursery because that second guava looks a bit lonely. In the meanwhile, you might want to change into some jeans because we'll be riding in my pick-up. How about it?"

"Sounds good," she said, without stopping to think.

"Great, then you get ready while I clean up the truck and I'll be back in five," he said. "I know a great spot across from the ocean where we can sit outside, have some burgers and fries, and talk. Does that give you enough time?"

"I'll be ready," she said.

This time I am.

A WOMAN OF
A CERTAIN AGE

Several months passed before Claudia Bennett decided to revisit her favorite art galleries located in the Chelsea section of Manhattan. It had been an excursion she and her late husband, Lance, enjoyed most Saturdays. They'd hail a taxi from their Upper West Side apartment and ride down to The Red Cat restaurant for lunch. Afterwards, they'd walk off the calories by strolling hand in hand along the avenues, making stops at the various art studios and shops that lined the streets. The couple had been about to celebrate their fortieth anniversary when Lance was the victim of a hit-and-run fatality. His last words to her before he left that day were about a special gift he was going to pick up for the occasion.

Fortunately, Lance had taken out a large insurance policy, one which had a double indemnity clause, and with the eventual sale of his software company, Claudia was more than well provided for.

Of course, money was no substitute for a loving husband, and Lance's death had all but devastated her. For weeks she was unable to leave the apartment until a trio of her dearest friends almost forcibly pried her out for a dinner date at a nearby restaurant on Columbus Avenue.

Claudia slowly began to accept other social invitations, and months later found herself entering The Red Cat for a nostalgic lunch. She waved to Earl, the bartender, and he smiled back acknowledging her presence. The restaurant was almost filled to capacity or she would have stopped to chat with him. The maître d' escorted her to a small, but comfortable, table where she had a full view of the bustling eatery. Earl had always sent complimentary espressos to Lance and her because they dined there so often. If the tables were occupied, they'd sit at the bar where he served them. Lance and he would talk baseball or basketball while Claudia checked the list of galleries they'd visit in the afternoon. The service and food at The Red Cat was superb, and Earl was always up on the latest exhibits. Today, on her first day back at the popular bistro, he not only sent over an espresso, but also a delicious-looking piece of apple cobbler, which she consumed in its entirety.

After Claudia finished her lunch and paid the bill, she stopped at the bar to speak with Earl, and to thank him for the lovely gesture.

"Hello Earl," she said. "Do you have a minute?"

"For you, Mrs. Bennett, always," he said. "It's a pleasure to see you. I heard about your husband. I'm so sorry. Mr. Bennett was a wonderful man. I know how much you must miss him. It's wonderful to see you out and about again."

"It feels good to be back. I wanted to thank you for the coffee and dessert, and your kind words. My husband always enjoyed our meals here, and particularly your Manhattans when we returned for Happy Hour."

"Ah, my specialty secret-ingredient Manhattan! So, where are you off to now?"

"I think it's time I started to check out the galleries again. Lance and I so enjoyed doing that together," she said, trying to sound upbeat.

"You definitely should. It's a beautiful day and you can always stop back for that cocktail or a glass of Chardonnay, on the house."

"Oh Earl, you have a great memory. Maybe another time. I'm off, and thanks again."

"Good bye, Mrs. Bennett. Enjoy your afternoon. Oh wait, I knew there was something I wanted to mention to you. The Bloodstone gallery reopened. It's called Carelli's now. That's the new owner's name. Nice guy, Italian. He's been in here once or twice. I may have his card…here it is. Yes, Carelli's. I haven't had a chance to see it yet, but I've heard from a few other diners that they've done a fabulous job remodeling the place."

"Wonderful. That'll be my first stop. Bloodstone's was Lance's favorite gallery. We even bought a small watercolor there a few years ago. Thanks for letting me know, and for everything. I guess I'll be a regular again," Claudia said, thinking that she would invite some of the girls along with her the next time.

Claudia exited onto Tenth Avenue and turned down Twenty-Third Street. It was a lengthy block, but one that was familiar to her. The sun was shining and she began to feel uplifted after a satisfying lunch and her short conversation with Earl. Lance would be proud that she'd begun to do things on her own again. They'd been a lucky couple in a traditional marriage, with two wonderful sons, both of whom became attorneys. Lance and she had been blessed with a group of caring friends, and now that she was ready to move on with her life, as her husband would have wanted, she'd begin to make plans with them other than the occasional dinner out.

When Claudia reached Carelli's, a handsome young man opened the double glass doors for her.

"Welcome to Carelli's, *Signora*. Is this your first visit?"

"My husband and I used to come here all the time when it was owned by Henry Bloodstone, but I just heard that there's a new owner. Would that be you?" she said.

"Alas, no. That would be Paolo Carelli. He's in the back office. Let me call him for you."

"No need to bother him. The gallery looks beautiful, so why don't I take a look around. Are you one of the artists by chance?"

"I did paint the walls if that counts," he said, with a charming smile.

"You did a very professional job," she said. "It looks fantastic. A great addition to the avenue."

"Since you knew the gallery before we took over, I'm sure you noticed that the Bloodstones never did much with the space, which is not to say that they didn't have a magnificent collection, but he was a strange sort. Kept to himself, either examining the inventory, or doing his own work. When he and his wife were ready to retire to Florida, he sold it to Paolo, whom he had met in Italy several years beforehand."

"You know, for all the times we visited here we never once met Mr. Bloodstone. We knew the manager, Nicole, quite well. Did she stay on with you?"

"Unfortunately not. Paolo told Nicole that the gallery wouldn't be ready for quite some time, and that as a new business we couldn't afford to keep paying her for the hiatus. Mr. Bloodstone had given her a handsome severance check, and I believe she's working at the gift store at the Metropolitan Museum. So now it's Mr. Carelli, and myself. Please forgive me, I am Bernardo Rigazzi."

"Ah, you are Italian! I thought I detected an accent," she said. "My name is Claudia Bennett."

"You are a perceptive woman, Mrs. Bennett," he said, as he bent to kiss her hand.

"And you are a flirtatious young man, Mr. Rigazzi!"

"How can I help it with such a gorgeous lady as yourself? Please, call me Bernardo."

Claudia began to feel happy and relaxed, and pleased to find out that Bernardo was knowledgeable about the artists in the gallery. They chatted amiably and before long, she told him about her husband's passing and the toll it had taken on her daily life, and he offered his condolences. While they were perusing the paintings, Bernardo began to look at her more closely, and with a strange curiosity. Suddenly, she became uncomfortable with the situation, and as she prepared to make a courteous exit, he offered an explanation as to the obvious change in climate.

"I'm sorry for staring, but I could swear I've seen you before today," he said, as if he'd read her mind. "I didn't mean to offend you, but you look so familiar."

"My husband and I were in this area all the time before he died; perhaps you saw us at another gallery," she said, breathing a sigh of relief that he hadn't meant to be rude, "but I think I would have remembered you."

"It wouldn't have been that because Paolo and I have been working almost nonstop renovating Carelli's for months, so we haven't visited the other galleries, although we've been meaning to. You know, to check out the competition. Luckily, my boss loves good food, so he and I have tried different restaurants in the neighborhood for lunch," he said. "That's the only time we take a break."

"Have you ever been to The Red Cat? Lance and I used to go there quite often. Perhaps you saw me there if you've been here that long."

"That must be it. Paolo and I like their menu, and the bartender is quite pleasant."

"It was our favorite lunch spot and my husband used to talk to Earl, that's the bartender's name, all the time. Oh, the two of them could go on and on about sports. I was just there today before I came here. Earl's the one who told me that your gallery had reopened."

"Then I owe him a million thanks for sending us such a beautiful lady."

"Oh goodness," Claudia said, clapping her palms together, "you're just what the doctor ordered for an old woman's ego."

"There's that crazy word you American women love to use…old!"

"Well, Bernardo, I usually don't tell nice young men how old I am, but I was just sixty-two," Claudia said, and hoped she wasn't blushing. She subconsciously smoothed down the back of her hair and gave him her most winning smile.

"We call that 'a woman of a certain age.' It's a beautiful time in a woman's life. She's secure, comfortable in her own skin, not out to impress anyone…mature, and forgive me, *bella*, very sexy."

"Oh, goodness! Thank you. No one's complimented me in quite a while, not since Lance."

"You must miss him very much," Bernardo said.

"Yes, I do. We had such a wonderful marriage, two beautiful children…but I'm sorry, I didn't mean to…" she said, searching her handbag for one of the linen handkerchiefs she always kept with her.

"No need to apologize. It shows the type of woman you are, caring and devoted. He was a lucky man. So tell me,"

Bernardo said, trying to lighten the mood, "what else do you do to keep busy besides driving young men crazy in art galleries."

Claudia laughed but before she had a chance to reply, an elegantly dressed man of about fifty walked briskly into the gallery space, carrying a sheaf of papers. He'd come from one of the back offices, and hadn't yet noticed Claudia. As soon as Bernardo realized his boss was there, he excused himself and rushed to join Mr. Paolo Carelli.

"I thought you were going to be finishing up in my office today. What are you doing out here that you're too busy to...Bernardo! Why didn't you tell me we had company?" he said, cutting short his question and softening his tone as he walked toward Claudia.

"Please excuse my outburst, *Signora*. I hope my 'decorator' isn't a bother. But now I understand why he'd rather be out here with you rather than finishing up the trim work in my office. Paolo Carelli, at your service," he said, with a bow.

"Claudia Bennett," she said, casually extending her hand, which he held in his for a brief moment before bringing it to his lips, as Bernardo had done.

"A pleasure, Mrs. Bennett. Bernardo, why didn't you call me out sooner to meet Mrs. Bennett?" he asked Bernardo, who had joined the twosome.

Not waiting for an answer, he continued.

"Please let us know if you're interested in any of the paintings, but in the meanwhile I hope you're enjoying the new gallery. May I offer you some coffee, Mrs. Bennett?"

"Oh, please call me Claudia, and I had an espresso over at The Red Cat before I came here. I hear you both know Earl."

"Paolo, Earl told Mrs. Bennett, I mean Claudia, about the gallery reopening and she was nice enough to stop in. I was showing her your collection, but perhaps I better finish up the work in the office now. Again, Claudia, it was lovely to meet you," Bernardo said, and began to walk toward the back area.

Claudia was beginning to feel uncomfortable for a second time because now Paolo was staring at her.

"Excuse me for looking right at you, but I have the eeriest feeling that I've seen you before," he said.

"Paolo," Bernardo cried out, stopping in his tracks. "I said the same thing. Claudia thinks we may have seen her at The Red Cat. She used to eat there all the time with her husband."

"Ah, so you're married. I should have suspected as much. A beautiful woman doesn't stay single for long."

"Claudia's husband passed away," Bernardo said quietly, so as not to upset her.

"Oh dear, I am very sorry to hear that. May I extend my sympathy to you?"

"Thank you, Paolo. I know my husband would have loved your gallery."

"If you don't mind, let's get back to the question of how we know you, and as much as I hate to admit it, Bernardo seems to be right. It must have been at the restaurant. Are you sure you wouldn't like some coffee? We have one of those machines in the back. It'll only take a minute. Perhaps a biscotti or a piece of chocolate?"

"Maybe some coffee, just black please. Earl already sent over a piece of their special cobbler at lunch today and it was enough for three people."

"Don't tell me you are like these silly women always worrying about their weight. No real man likes skinny girls. I bet your husband thought you were perfect. Come on now, Claudia, you can't refuse a little sweet with your coffee. Bernardo, please get it ready—we'll all have some."

"I see I can't fight you, so I'll forget about my diet for

today," Claudia said, obviously relishing the exchange and the attention. She prided herself on her appearance and was grateful that she'd chosen an elegant, but casual, outfit for today's outing.

"I'm on it, Paolo," Bernardo said, using a popular American expression while making his way toward the kitchen.

"Wait!" Paolo said, his hands flying above his head.

"What is it, boss? Do you want me here or making coffee?"

"Stay here for one minute more and tell me if I'm dreaming, but isn't there a portrait in the back warehouse of a woman in a yellow dress, and specifically, a woman who looks exactly like Claudia Bennett!"

"That's it. That's where we know you from," Bernardo said.

"Where? What portrait?" Claudia said, looking and sounding confused.

"Henry Bloodstone left a few of his own paintings here for us to sell, and that portrait was one of them. Let me bring it out because you won't believe it until you see it for yourself. I'll be right back. Do you have some time to wait?" Paolo said.

"Of course, how could I leave now?" she said, thinking about a yellow dress that Lance had chosen for her on one of their shopping trips.

"Please Bernardo, offer our guest a seat and then make the coffee, although we'll probably need something stronger to help figure out this mystery," Paolo said and headed toward the back warehouse.

Bernardo led Claudia to a tiled-top table and excused himself. Claudia took out her phone and looked at the photos of her beloved husband. There were several of him alone, and more of the two of them together. There was one photo of her wearing the yellow dress, and now the two men said there was a portrait of someone who looked like her in the same outfit.

Oh Lance, how you would have appreciated the goings on here. Paolo and Bernardo are true gentlemen—so kind and making me feel like a princess in a fairy tale, even if I am sixty-two. And they have the most delightful accents, and those wonderful European manners. Now one of them is brewing coffee, and the other is in the back because he swears there's a portrait of me in their inventory. It's really like a scene out of a movie. Alfred Hitchcock or Woody Allen, or a combination of both.

"Claudia!" Paolo yelped, "Here! See for yourself. It's you."

Claudia's jaw dropped as she looked at the picture Paolo held up. She had no words other than what he had already declared. It was a painting of her.

"Oh my goodness…it looks exactly like me…and that yellow dress…but how…" she stuttered, barely able to get the words out.

Bernardo joined them at the table where he placed the cups and saucers, alongside a serving tray of the promised sweets. Once he poured coffee, with a splash of Sambuca, he looked up at the painting, and then back at Claudia.

"So, I think we all agree that it is you," Bernardo said, and continued with as much arrogance as he dared muster up in front of his boss. "I may have the solution. Is it possible that before your husband died he could have commissioned it from the Bloodstone gallery before Paolo took it over? Maybe as a surprise for you?"

"Dear me, now I have to agree that my associate is correct. It is quite common for husbands or wives to bring in a photograph, and then have the gallery commission a portraitist. In this case, the gallery owner did it himself. Look here at his famous signature, Hb. Not even the full name, but everyone in the art world knows it's Henry Bloodstone."

Claudia, her legs wobbly and her breath coming in short spurts, sat at the table and took a sip of the strong coffee fortified with sweet Italian liquor. It burned slightly going down, but it shocked her system, and things began to fall into place.

"Maybe that was what my husband meant. Let me explain. Our fortieth anniversary was coming up, and Lance teased that he was going to surprise me with a gift. Something special. Those were his last words to me before the accident," she said, beginning to tear up. "And like I told you, we did come to the gallery all the time when the Bloodstones owned it. Lance particularly admired his work. Yes, I think what Bernardo suggests is right. Here, look at this picture of me in that dress."

Both men looked at the phone, and nodded their heads in agreement.

"Claudia, I didn't mean to make you sad, but you had to see this for yourself. It's definitely you," Paolo said softly.

"The yellow dress, it was Lance's favorite."

"Paolo, surely there must be some paperwork in the office on the paintings that Bloodstone left here," Bernardo said. "Shall I go see what I can find?"

"Bouna fortuna! Good luck. He kept terrible records—everything on little slips of paper. Thanks be to the saints that he only left a half-dozen or so of his signed work in our inventory because he didn't want to have to send them to Florida. We had already purchased some of what you see in the gallery when we bought the business, but those are all from various other artists. Our agreement was that if anything more of his sold, we would forward him a check after keeping a small commission to cover packing and shipping."

"Then we can settle this right now. Why don't you call the Bloodstones, and see what he says?" Bernardo said, handing Paolo his phone.

175

"One more good idea from Bernardo and I'll be forced to give him a raise, but let's end the suspense. I'll call him," he said, punching in the number. "Please, Claudia, take a cookie...you look a little pale. Henry? There you are. It's me, Paolo. *Molto bene, grazie.* And you? Good. I need to ask you something about a picture you left. Do you remember a portrait of a very elegant looking lady in a yellow dress? No, you didn't leave any paper work on it," Paolo said, rolling his eyes and gesturing disbelief with a wave of his hand. "Did someone commission that? Yes? Can you email me the particulars? There's nothing in the files. Why? Because there is a lovely woman here, who we are about to make very happy. Yes, of course, the woman in the picture."

Paolo was silent for a moment before continuing.

"I see. I'll explain all that, but send me the figures anyway so I have it for my files. Don't worry, I'll take care of the business end. That's why you retired, remember? Take care! *Ciao!*"

Along with nibbling on a few cookies, Claudia and Bernardo had listened to every word of the one-sided conversation, and now waited for proof about Bernardo's suggested scenario.

"My dear Mrs. Claudia Bennett, your husband did indeed commission a portrait of you from Mr. Bloodstone himself. He'd given Henry a couple of photos of you in the yellow dress, but Henry had lost your husband's cell phone number, which is no surprise seeing how disorganized he is with everything else, so had no way to reach him. He wasn't too worried because he figured Mr. Bennett would return to pick up the painting on the appointed date. Unfortunately, that day must have been when the horrible accident occurred that took your husband's life. After that, the Bloodstones sold us the business and retired."

Claudia put her head down on the table and quietly wept while the two men looked at her with compassion.

"Claudia, I know this is a shock, but please don't cry. Your husband loved you. He wanted to immortalize you in this portrait. What man wouldn't want to do that for you? Come now, don't be sad. It was a beautiful gesture, and now you have the portrait that he planned for you," Bernardo said. "Surely you'd like to have it."

Claudia looked up and smiled through her tears.

"Yes, Bernardo, of course I want it. I was so blessed to be married to a man like that. What a beautiful gift he left for me," she said, looking closely at the portrait. "It's a little large to take with me so would you mind delivering it to my apartment? I'd be happy to pay for any handling charges," she said.

"Of course, and I'll hang it properly also," Bernardo said. "We would never charge for that."

"Claudia, I don't like to bring this up, but Mr. Bennett only left a deposit. Five thousand dollars. Henry just told me that the balance in the same amount was due upon pick-up. Henry will never issue a refund of the deposit, and if you take the portrait, he expects to be paid. Otherwise, he wants me to ship it to him in Florida," Paolo said, "or try to sell it to someone else. How could we even think about doing that!"

"I definitely want it, and I'd be happy to pay the balance to Mr. Bloodstone. I'm sorry I didn't even ask about a payment, but I have a check with me today. Can you give me his address?"

"Please make it out to Carelli's, and I'll send Henry a business check, which he prefers. Now, just between us, and please don't tell your friends, but Henry's a sucker for a good romance, and your husband must have softened up that old goat's hide when he mentioned your anniversary. I've never seen a Bloodstone portrait go for ten thousand. They're usually at least double and even triple that amount," Paolo said, hoping to make Claudia feel secure in the purchase while being honest in his assessment.

"I understand. Lance loved me in that dress. He must have taken dozens of pictures of me in it. I only wish he could have seen the completed portrait. Wait a minute. What if I brought you some photos of him? Could you send them on to Mr. Bloodstone to do another portrait? Then I could hang both as a pair," she said, taking out her check-book. "Do you think he'd do it?"

"I'm sure he'll accept the commission. He just told me he's getting a little bored in Boca with golf and what he calls 'condo commandos.' And, I'll tell him that he must give you the same good deal he gave to Mr. Bennett. No funny monkey business," Paolo said, making Claudia laugh with the slang term.

"Wonderful. I'll stop by tomorrow with the photos. Shall I write you a check for the balance due on my paint-ing, and a deposit for Lance's?"

"Yes, thank you, but I'm going to double check with Henry later to confirm. I can let you know tomorrow when you come back with the photos. I'll hold the check until then, and we'll write up a proper receipt for you."

Claudia made out a check for ten thousand dollars, and took a deep breath. Her fortieth wedding anniversary couldn't be shared with the love of her life, but it would not go unobserved. She'd always have the pair of paintings to remember him by.

"I'm so glad I stopped in here today, but I should be get-ting home. Why don't we wait for the new painting, so that Bernardo doesn't have to make two trips."

"Of course. That's no problem at all," Bernardo said. "I can help you find a taxi now if you're ready."

"Yes, thank you. Paolo, Bernardo, today has been the first day I've really smiled since Lance died," she said.

"Our pleasure, I'm sure. See you tomorrow then. Bernardo, you can finally finish up in my office after you hail a cab for Claudia. *Ciao!*"

After Bernardo left with Claudia, Paolo began to stack the coffee cups and saucers while singing *"O Sole Mio."* He was very happy, as was Claudia. And Bernardo.

Bernardo opened the heavy glass doors as he'd done earlier in the day for Claudia Bennett and walked over to the table to help clear the dishes.

"Nah, I got it," Paolo said, in a tone indistinguishable from the fine continental accent he'd used with Claudia only moments ago. "That was quick, Bernie."

"Yeah, Paulie," he said, sounding like a common thug. "There was a taxi right outside."

Paolo/Paulie looked at the check and smiled as he showed it to Bernardo/Bernie.

"Not bad for a couple hour's work, my friend. That prison they stuck you in musta had some great art classes. You're pretty damn good. And the yellow dress was the clincher," said Paulie, now immersed in familiar street talk.

"Hey, I told you it paid to let me eat at The Red Cat. That's where all those rich 'women of a certain age' hang out. I spotted Claudia right away, eatin' that sauce and not droppin' a bit on her fancy yellow dress. She never even noticed me sketching her and her husband didn't either. And we have Earl to thank for calling and tipping us off about her being a widow. You were right figuring she'd be back here sooner or later. So, Paulie, who was Henry Bloodstone today?"

"My voicemail, as usual."

"It's a good thing Bloodstone moved to one of those islands, Santa something or other. No one will ever find him and he doesn't want to be found. Said he was sick of cell phones and all the rest of the New York bullshit."

"Hey, watch the language."

"Geez, it's only the two of us. I'm careful around our customers. You know, Paulie,

I almost cracked up when you used that Boca story. That's the last place Bloodstone would end up in."

"True enough but we don't have to worry about him anymore. He's gone for good. What a crappy business man—sold us this place for a song."

"Yeah, a bit of white paint slapped on the walls, a few lights and it's a hot spot. It certainly impressed Claudia," Bernie said. "She's a nice lady. Real classy and not like some of those other stuck-up broads who come in here. I kinda feel guilty taking money from her."

Paulie wiped down the table before addressing his partner.

"Why should you feel guilty? Let me tell you something. Loneliness is a terrible thing. We helped that lady today by giving her something her husband never would have thought of. Who knows what he was going to surprise her with, probably another piece of jewelry, but now she'll have a pair of 'Bloodstone' portraits for their fortieth anniversary, and when her fancy friends see it, they'll be flocking in here for their original Bloodstones. At ten or twenty thousand a pop, they'll think they're getting the deal of the century," Paulie said, pocketing the check.

"I guess you're right, but one day I want to sign my own name to those portraits, and not that stupid Hb."

Paulie sighed because he knew he'd have to once again explain the business plan to his associate.

"Listen, Bernie, we're making a pile of dough with the operation just the way it is. Buying this old gallery from Bloodstone and fixing it up was the best thing I ever did, and you get half the profits because your paintings keep getting better all the time. Actually, I think you're more talented than the great Henry Bloodstone himself, but why use your name when you're such an expert forger? Even down to his initials. Unfortunately, the name of Bernie Capp is only well known at the Elmira Correctional Facility, where you were recently a guest. I gotta say though, this angle worked out pretty good today, and the anniversary bit was a bonus, but we can't sit around and wait for people to die. We better go back to pulling the other scam. How's that canvas coming along of Mrs. Brittany?"

"Just about done. I'll stick it in the window a couple of days from now, and tell Earl to drop a few hints about the gallery and the picture he saw that looks just like her next time she's in the restaurant and we'll nail it. Of course, I made a few adjustments. I took out the wrinkles and jowls because old age don't sell so good around here."

"Bernie, how about we go on making people happy and padding our bank accounts. Let's head over to The Red Cat for a drink to celebrate and give Earl his cut."

The two men locked up and left for the day, confident that no one would ever find out about their unlawful business practices. It almost worked until the day Henry Bloodstone got tired of island living and came back to town, unannounced, and was surprised to see paintings in the window of Carelli's with his signature on them.

COFFEE BREAK

"Has Audrey been in yet, Jan?" Roy said, his eyes scanning the room.

Jan Reynolds ran Jan's Place, the popular coffee shop located in the atrium of the Harbor View Independent Living Residence.

"You just missed her, darn it, and she had to hurry because Mr. Joel needed her back in Admissions pronto," Jan said. "She ordered her usual, which I packed to go. I can't believe you guys keep missing each other."

Jan was a natural born matchmaker, and she'd been trying to get Audrey and Roy together since he began his job as a lab technician a couple of months ago. Unfortunately, the two worked on different floors, so there was little chance that they'd run into each other in the hallways of the large establishment.

"What did she order today?" Roy said, wanting to know every detail about the petite redhead he'd been admiring, but was too shy to approach.

"Like I said, her usual. Iced coffee with skimmed milk and a piece of our low-fat apple cake, not that she has to watch her figure," Jan said.

"I guess I'll have the same," Roy said, with a sigh so loud and long that the gentleman seated nearby looked up fearing someone had fainted.

"You okay over there, Roy?" Mr. Louis said. Mr. Louis was approaching ninety, but his eyesight and hearing were perfect. Nothing got past him. "You mooning over that cute gal with the red curls?"

Roy blushed a shade deeper than Audrey's titian hair before addressing Mr. Louis.

"I'm okay, sir. Just taking a breather," he said.

"You can't fool me. I know when you young guys are in love. I may be old, but I still have an eye for the ladies," Mr. Louis said.

"You better keep that to yourself because I see your current flame coming down the hall to meet you," Jan said.

"Oh now, Jan, you know I'm a one-woman man, but it doesn't hurt to look," he said, and moved his newspaper to an empty chair to make room for company.

Jan prepared the coffee and dessert exactly the way she did for Audrey, and served it to Roy. He sipped the cold beverage and wrinkled up his nose.

This would taste a whole lot better if it were hot and with cream, he thought, careful not to sigh again. *But I'm going to drink it anyway. Maybe it'll help me channel up enough courage to talk to her. The cake is great, so I could always tell her we have something in common, like dessert.*

"You know, I could fix you guys up," Jan said, breaking into his reverie. "You're perfect for each other, even if you are a head taller."

"No, thank you!" he said. "I know you're itching to get involved, but I've got to do this my own way."

The next day Roy took his break from the lab earlier than usual, and hoped he'd be on time to catch Audrey. When he spotted Jan, she told him that the girl of his dreams probably wouldn't be in because she'd stopped by earlier in the day. Dejected, Roy sat at the counter instead of taking up one of the tables, and again ordered Audrey's favorites. His break would be over before he knew it and there was still no sign of her.

Roy thought about asking Jan to do some groundwork for him, or at least to dial his extension when Audrey was there, but decided against it. He didn't want to be reminded of his mother trying to fix him up on blind dates when he was still in school. He'd always been bashful around girls and aside from one or two casual girlfriends, he'd really never been in love. At least, not until now.

"She's quite the popular gal—always joking around with everyone, but respectful. Come to think of it, it's rare that she sits by herself," Jan said, placing Roy's order in front of him unaware that she was dampening his spirits. "You've got to be more positive if you want to meet her."

"How can I approach her when she's surrounded by people?" Roy shot back. "What if she's dating her boss, that unbearable Mr. Joel? She's probably never even noticed me and I can't sit around all afternoon waiting for her. I'll get fired, and then have no girl and no job."

"Okay, Mr. Negative, enjoy your snack," Jan said. "You be sure to let me know when you need my help and I'll make it happen."

Jan set about brewing a fresh urn of coffee and went into the kitchen to prepare a tray of desserts. Business was thriving with employees and residents making time for a leisurely cup of coffee, a sandwich, or one of her specialty muffins. Jan knew most of the socializing at Harbor View took place in her café; getting Audrey and Roy together would be child's play if only Roy would let her handle the arrangements.

Just at that moment, Audrey raced into the coffee shop. Roy, who had about five minutes left on his break, was deep into his book and didn't notice her.

"Excuse me, everyone," she said. No one minded the distraction because even with all the entertainment available to the residents, Jan's Place was still the favorite for casual get-togethers, and a little light-hearted gossip. "I think I left my cell phone here this morning. Would someone mind dialing it for me? It's pink and the number is…"

"No need," Roy called out from his counter seat, his face still planted in the book. "There's a fancy pink phone under the menu. I was going to leave it for Jan." He held up the phone in his outstretched arm without turning around.

This scatterbrained woman can walk over to me and take back her property without disturbing my last few minutes of peace, he thought, annoyed at the intrusion.

"Well, thank you," she said to the faceless stranger. Audrey wanted to tell the man holding up the phone how appreciative she was, but not when he didn't have the decency to turn and greet her eye to eye. She grabbed the phone and started to leave when she spied what was on the placemat before the man. Iced coffee and her favorite low-fat apple cake.

"Did you add skim milk to that coffee?" she said, not caring if she was interrupting his reading. If he could be rude, so could she.

"As a matter of fact…" Roy began to say as he swung around to face the ditzy person who'd forgotten her phone. When he saw Audrey, he became tongue tied. "Uh, skim milk…milk…yes, I think so. I don't know."

"You don't know?" she said, trying not to sound hostile because he was sort of cute, in a dorky kind of way. She'd seen him a few times, but figured he was married or involved because except for a couple of furtive glances, he'd never said a word to her.

While the two stared at each other, Jan came out of the kitchen holding a platter of cranberry scones. She knew there was a big meeting about to break and the executive team would be in soon asking for their favorites.

"I see you two have finally met," Jan said, after placing the tray in the tiered glass case.

"We haven't exactly met, but this gentleman found my cell phone. We don't know each other, and I'm not sure I want to," Audrey said, her nose in the air.

Roy held on to the phone and sat as still as a statue while trying to come up with an apology, but he was speechless. Audrey was so vivacious, and he'd acted like a fool. He knew he had to say something before she left, which she was about to. She'd never want to get to know him if he didn't speak up.

"Cream. I like heavy cream in my coffee," he managed to mumble. "Hot. Hot coffee. I don't even like iced coffee," he blurted out, embarrassed that he couldn't put two words together.

"Then why on earth use skim milk? Or drink it cold? I hope these questions aren't too difficult for you," she said, in a joking manner this time. She realized he was shy and didn't want to embarrass him, although it was probably too late for that.

Again, Roy had no words. He was mesmerized by her

large, tawny eyes that had a gleam in them, but he wasn't sure it was for him.

"Oh, stop fooling around and introduce yourselves. You think I have time for this nonsense? The folks who run this place are coming in any minute, and I've got to get their coffee ready or they'll fall asleep at the table. Audrey, be nice, and Roy, stand up when a lady talks to you, or better yet, invite her to join you. And Audrey, if the cat's got your tongue, it'll be the first time since I've known you. I've got work to do," Jan said, pretending to be annoyed although it was easy to see through her charade.

By this time, everyone in the café was engaged in the couple's conversation and waited for the next installment.

"Audrey, I'm Roy. It's nice to meet you," he said, rising from the stool. "Would you care to join me? I'm sorry I was impolite before, but I'm so caught up in this book I forgot my manners."

"That's okay," she said, a smile crossing her face. "I guess I was a little gruff also. I love to read, so you are forgiven."

"Won't you sit down?" he said, forgetting that he was due at the lab.

"I've got to get back to the office. Admissions is crazy, and I told Mr. Joel I was only going to pop over here to see if I'd left my phone, and he can be a total pain if I'm two minutes late," Audrey said, not wanting to end their meeting.

"How about dinner tonight?" Roy said, encouraged that Mr. Joel was seemingly out of the picture.

"I'd like that," she said. "Why don't you give me a call and we'll set it up."

"Great idea. Will do. Speak to you later then," he said.

On her way out, Jan said, "Audrey, aren't you forgetting something?"

"Hey, Jan's right," said Mr. Louis, not missing a trick. "He doesn't have your number, and you forgot your phone again."

Roy was still clutching the pink phone when Audrey walked over to the counter.

"I'll trade you," she said. "You give me back my phone, and I'll write down my number for you. Deal?"

"Deal," he said.

After they exchanged information, Audrey left to return to her office. Roy was about to finish his cake when Jan brought over a steaming cup of coffee in a to-go cup.

"I added some cream for you," she said. "Now get out of here before they come looking for you. And I appreciate the fact that you made my job easier—getting you two together, that is."

Roy paid the check, and thanked Jan. As he walked out of the café, Mr. Louis had the last word.

"You take that young lady to a nice restaurant tonight, and bring her some flowers," he said, and went back to holding court with the other residents.

PICTURE YOU AND ME

"Hazel! I thought you'd never get here. Sorry your flight was so late. Welcome to New York! Come on in," Geneva said, as she leaned forward to give her older sister a hug. "It's been ages. Let me take your bags. How's Steve? The kids?"

"Hello, Geneva. Please, give me a minute to take off my coat before the interrogation. I'm exhausted. Flying is impossible these days and the airport was busier than ever. I was up at the crack of dawn to leave myself enough time only to have a three-hour delay on the runway," Hazel said, stepping into Geneva's loft.

"Oh, that's such a drag, but you're here now. That's all that matters. Thank you for coming. It means a lot to me."

"I'm sure it does. It took me forever to rearrange my schedule," Hazel said. "Do you have a guest room in this... this loft? Or do I camp out on the floor? Lord, this place is tremendous. Where's all your artwork? That is why I'm here, isn't it?"

"The gallery picked up most of the pieces yesterday to prepare for my show tonight. Did you see the portrait?" Geneva said, pointing to a picture that hung on the otherwise bare wall. A few large abstract paintings sat on the floor leaning against a long table, but only the beautifully framed portrait of the sisters held a place of honor.

"How could I miss it? It sticks out like a sore thumb in here."

"Oh, it does not. Don't be such a grump. You're an incredible portraitist and this one is my favorite of all your work...because it's of us," Geneva said, trying to get a smile out of her sister. The compliment wasn't false. Hazel was a masterful artist.

"That was a long time ago. A lot of good that does me now. No one wants portraits anymore. The only time I even see one is on television, *Modern Family*, and that's not the kind of work I do," Hazel said.

"I didn't know you watched that show. I'm hooked on it," Geneva said, trying to find common ground.

"Yes, Gen, it happens to be one of my favorites. What did you think I watched? Lawrence Welk reruns? I'm not that out of it even though I don't live in the big city."

Seeing that any hope of a meaningful conversation was out of the question, Geneva took Hazel's tote bags, and pointed to the far end of the roomy loft. Behind French doors fitted with linen drapery was a bedroom connecting to its own high-tech bathroom. The platform bed, low to the floor, was flanked by two nightstands holding stainless-steel gooseneck lamps. A dresser, with a matching oval mirror, and a small upholstered chair filled out the rest of the room.

"Is this okay for you?" Geneva said, leading her sister to the bedroom.

Hazel looked back at the large expanse of the loft, and aside from an open kitchen and another bathroom, she didn't notice a second bedroom. This was the first time she'd seen Geneva's new living quarters since her divorce from Mac.

"This must be your bedroom," Hazel said. "I don't want to put you out."

"The couch in the living room is so comfortable that I usually end up falling asleep on it anyway. I'll be fine and I thought you'd prefer your privacy," Geneva said, trying to be agreeable to her older sister, who still looked peeved.

"It's a good thing I'm short. How in the world do you get down into bed?" Hazel said, looking up at her younger, but much taller, sister.

"I'm used to it. It's no biggie. Why don't you put your stuff away? The closet's pretty roomy, and I'll make us some coffee. Take your time, we don't have to be at the gallery till seven," Geneva said and whisked herself out of the room, not wanting to hear any further gripes her sister might have.

"I only drink decaf now," Hazel called out to Geneva, who had just made it into the kitchen.

Geneva was about to pour fresh water into the coffee maker, but stopped in her tracks and turned back toward the bedroom to find out about this latest change in her sister's lifelong coffee habit.

"What about the French Roast that you live on? I bought it especially for you, and it's delicious...much better than the store brand I usually buy. Since when do you drink decaf? We're a caffeinated family," she said, trying to lighten the moment.

"When you get breast cysts, then we'll see who starts to drink decaf," Hazel said, "not that I wish that on you."

"Oh, I'm so sorry. I didn't know. Why didn't you ever mention that to me, for heaven's sakes? What did the doctor say?" Geneva said.

"It's nothing serious, but she advised giving up caffeine because sometimes that can be the cause of the problem. I didn't want to worry you. You're always so busy. And yes, the cysts went away in about six weeks after I made the change. I was lucky," Hazel said, her eyes tearing up.

"You should have told me. I'm glad it didn't turn into something serious, but you should have told me anyway," Geneva said, irritated that her sister didn't feel the need to share a personal health matter with her.

Hazel finished unpacking, grabbed a tissue from the bathroom, and sighed.

"I'll call you the next time I sneeze. Satisfied?"

"Oh, Hazel. You're so tough sometimes. Come on, let's go down to Cookie's Cafe. Nikki will be there today and I want you to meet her. She's the boss's daughter, and a sweetheart. We can get one of those fancy drinks, decaf of course, and they have the most delicious baked goods."

Hazel finished putting her cosmetics in the bathroom vanity drawer, and the two women walked out of the bedroom, arm in arm.

"Sure, you eat a piece of cake and maybe you'll go from a size four to a four and a half. Me? One crumb, one pound. How did my little sister get to be six inches taller than me? You have all that extra room. It's not fair," Hazel said, and finally laughed.

Nikki was clearing off tables and greeting patrons at the coffee shop, seemingly all at once. Geneva and Hazel seated themselves at a corner booth, and Nikki gave them a wave and motioned that she'd be right over.

"Hello ladies," Nikki said, as she arrived at their table. "I bet this is your sister, Hazel. Gen's been talking about you all week. It's totally awesome that you made it up for her big show."

"It's nice to meet you, Nikki. Yes, I'm very pleased about the exhibit tonight," Hazel said, sounding less than enthusiastic.

"Could we get two decafs, please," Geneva said, "unless you want a cappuccino."

"Thank you, no. A cup of decaf would be fine," Hazel said.

"Decaf for sure," Nikki said, arching an eyebrow. She'd never known Geneva to order anything other than a super-strong double espresso.

"And skim milk, if it's no trouble," Hazel added.

"Not at all. Oh, Gen, We're out of Dad's lemon meringue pie that you like, but we have some dynamite pistachio biscotti and chocolate macaroons. I'll bring over a sampler plate," Nikki said, and departed to take another order before heading back to the kitchen.

"I see you get the royal treatment here. Nice to have your own personal server," Hazel said. "She even knows what your favorites are."

"When Nikki sees me, she automatically brings out a few things, and frankly, it's all delicious so I don't really have any favorites, except the pie she mentioned. Luke is her dad and the boss, and when I first started painting, he let me hang a few pictures to sell on consignment. Customers liked the fact that a local artist did them and they began to buy whatever was on the walls. Since then, Luke's stopped charging me because of the commission the art brings in," Geneva said, slightly annoyed since she'd told her sister the exact scenario many times over the phone.

"Ah yes, now I remember. The Bakery Artist I believe *New York Magazine* called you."

"I was lucky that their food editor comes in here all the time and she passed it on for one of their columns. That's all it was. Luck," Geneva said, trying to sound modest.

"Yes, luck seems to follow you everywhere. It followed you the day you left your husband and picked up a paintbrush for the first time in your life."

"It was therapy for me. It was pretty devastating when Mac and I ended our marriage," Geneva said, feeling the harshness of her sister's words.

"Then why'd you break up?" Hazel asked.

Before Geneva could answer, Nikki arrived with the decafs, desserts, and a pitcher of skim milk, all carefully balanced on a round tray.

"Here you go. Anything else?" Nikki said.

"No thanks, we're fine. You can leave the check any time," Geneva said, like she always did even knowing that they'd never accept payment.

"Everything's on the house today. Two artists in the same family, that's what I call special. I'm coming to your opening tonight with a few friends," the young server said. "See you later and good luck, but you don't need it. You'll sell all your stuff, for sure. Oh, Dad said if you have any extras he'd be glad to hang them here."

"I'm sure I have some smaller paintings in storage. I'll get them down here next week," Geneva said.

"Great. Just wave if you need me," Nikki said, and scooted to the entrance to help seat a few patrons.

"So, where were we?" Geneva said.

"Mac. You. Divorce. Why?" Hazel said, sounding like an attorney cross-examining a witness.

"Because fifteen years of an unhappy marriage was enough for both of us. The split was mutual."

"If you were so unhappy, why are you two still so close?"

It had been a long time since the two sisters had come

anywhere near to having a heart-to-heart talk, and Geneva felt it was her chance to explain things the way they actually were.

"Mac and I are best friends. Always have been, but we weren't good as husband and wife. Our marriage wasn't like yours. We never had what you and Steve do," Geneva said.

"You should have worked a little harder at it."

"Is that what you and Steve do? Work at your marriage? It never looked that way to me," Geneva said, with an edge to her voice.

"I guess my good luck was with my husband and the kids. But it's not all fun and games," Hazel said, picking at a piece of one of the biscotti. "We have our share of problems, like every other married couple."

"Your kids are the greatest," Geneva said.

"You could have had your own, that family you wanted."

Geneva didn't know if she could go on to reveal the source of the insurmountable issue in her marriage.

All my friends are aware of the situation I was in, even Nikki, but this is Manhattan where people accept most anything. Sometimes Hazel is so judgmental, but it seems that she's interested in finding out more about the divorce and my relationship with Mac.

Geneva took a chance and plunged ahead.

"Mac and I didn't screw enough for me to get pregnant," she began, more abruptly than planned.

"Gen, really. I don't need to know your personal business," Hazel said.

Geneva realized she should have tempered her opening remark, but it was too late to detour from the subject.

"Why not? We're sisters. You should be my best friend, not Mac. I tried to talk to you about my marriage so many times, but you never listened."

"You better listen to me now," Hazel said. "I have a few years on you, but anyone in a good marriage will tell you the same thing. Marriage isn't only about sex. Steve and I don't spend all our time in the bedroom."

"I'm not only talking about sex. Of course, there's more to marriage but when sex isn't there at all, it sure doesn't help matters," Geneva said, shoving half a macaroon in her mouth so she wouldn't have to answer any more questions. The two sat in silence while they sipped their coffee.

"Couldn't you have had an affair with some guy and stayed married?" Hazel said.

"I can't believe you said that. But even if you meant it, which I know you didn't, no, I couldn't have. It wasn't only the sex. There were other things," Geneva said, beginning to regret that she'd brought up the situation. Maybe Hazel wasn't ready to accept knowing anything more about Mac and her.

"Enough to toss away fifteen years? Especially if your husband is your best friend? Do you know how many women would love to say that? I have to admit, you two would have made beautiful children," Hazel said. "And I'm sorry for making that crack about the affair. I know that's not your style. I wish you had discussed all this with me before you ran off to a divorce lawyer. I could have helped, or you could have gone for marriage counseling. It seems like such a shame for two decent people to split up."

"When I tried to talk to you about my marriage you changed the subject. All we discussed was decorating, gardening—anything to avoid hearing what I had to say. Then when my life is falling apart, you're off to the mall to look for a new blouse for your green leggings for the next charity event. Nothing I had to tell you was important enough to keep you on the phone. Even the mall is more pressing than listening to your sister," Geneva said.

"How do you remember all this trivia? And I would never wear green leggings, anywhere. Who am I? Peter Pan?

I certainly would have listened if you told me something was wrong, but there's always something wrong. You're such a drama queen. I'll never understand why you didn't become an actress."

"I actually thought about it, but I hate studying and would have had too much trouble learning lines. That's why I turned to art. Lines don't matter for me," Geneva said, hoping for a compliment on her work.

"Obviously, but it would explain why you barely stumbled through college," Hazel said, once more on the offensive.

"We both know I'm no genius. You don't have to rub it in. Anyway, I started to tell you something before. You're not the only one who thought I should have stayed in my marriage. Fifteen years is a long time, and Mac is a terrific guy, but I want to spend the rest of my life with the right person, not just a friend. And, speaking of men, there is something I have to tell you. You're going to meet a young man tonight at the opening. His name is Jake. Nikki introduced us," Geneva said, signaling for more coffee.

"An artist? A critic? Nikki introduced you? Who is he, another one of her relatives?"

"He's my boyfriend, and a friend of hers."

Nikki arrived with two fresh cups of decaf, but seeing the disgruntled look on her customers' faces, she placed the coffees in front of them without a word and quickly cleared away the used mugs. As soon as she left, Hazel picked up where they left off.

"Now that's something I would have stayed home from the mall to hear. I didn't even know you were dating. Wait a minute. The name Jake isn't exactly from our age range, and he's a friend of Nikki's? Just how old is this young man?" Hazel said, pouring the last of the milk into her coffee.

"Twenty-five."

"Oh, my God. It's a good thing I'm drinking decaf

because I'd have a heart attack along with the breast cysts if this had any caffeine in it. Gen, you're a forty year old cliché. You leave a good marriage…" Hazel began to say before her sister cut her off.

"It wasn't a good marriage," she said softly.

"Move to a loft, which I'm sure Mac is paying for, start painting, and take up with a kid," Hazel continued on as if she hadn't heard Geneva's last remark.

"Jake's more than a kid. I felt dead before I met him."

"Oh, please. You didn't look so dead to me."

"I meant inside. Didn't you ever guess? Mac is gay," Geneva said, finally blurting it out.

"Oh for Pete's sake, you're not a cliché, you're a freaking mini-series. How could I have ever guessed about Mac? You two always looked so, so…right together. I just assumed your marriage was like mine, and that kids would come. I'm sorry, I mean I'm not sorry if it's the best thing for him and you, but I simply can't believe it, and neither will Steve. Oh wait, I think my husband suspected, but I told him he was dead wrong. Looks like my husband has gaydar. Oh, sorry again, I can't even believe I know that word, probably from Cameron and Mitch."

"Mac and I looked good together because he did all the shopping," Geneva said, as a way to break the tension although it was true. "But Jake is sweet and sexy, and we have fun together. He doesn't care that I'm older. I mean, fifteen years isn't huge," Geneva said, trying not to sound defensive.

"You look good now, but what about ten years from now? Will he still not care about the age difference or those gray hairs? You need a touch-up, by the way."

"It's not like that," Geneva said, ignoring the remark about her hair. "He's not my soul mate and I don't plan on marrying him. For right now, it's a nice, easy relationship."

"Soul mate? If you wait for that you'll still be in your

overalls instead of a wedding dress and no, you can't borrow mine unless you want to walk down the aisle in a mini with your butt hanging out," Hazel said.

Geneva set her coffee cup down, but not before sputtering out what little liquid she hadn't yet swallowed. After coughing and clearing her throat, she began to laugh.

"Good one! Hazel, do you realize that this is probably the longest conversation we've had in years?"

"You can be exasperating, but actually, you're right. And I might be partially to blame for that. Not for everything, mind you, but for putting you off at times," Hazel said, handing Geneva a napkin.

"I'm telling you about Jake now because I didn't want it to be a surprise tonight when you meet him. He's very affectionate. It embarrassed me at first, but I like it. I need it," she said.

"Yes, the younger people are like that," Hazel mused. "The kids are always hugging each other and us, and all their friends hug us too. Not like our generation. Did we ever hear 'I love you' from Mom or Dad?"

"Only at the end when Dad was in the hospital. I told him I loved him and he said it back. I was holding his hand when he died. I don't remember ever hearing it from Mom."

"You and Mac were wonderful caregivers. I'm sorry I wasn't here more for you, and them," Hazel said. "The kids were so young and Steve was busy establishing his law practice, but I still should have made the time to be here, not dump it all on you."

"Hazel, don't beat yourself up over that. Mac and I lived nearby, and it was easier for us to handle everything. You called me every day to find out how things were going," Geneva said, "and you, Steve, and the kids came up for the funeral services."

"Let's get back to your Jake," Hazel said, feeling guilty

that she'd left all the funeral arrangements, a year apart, for both their parents to her younger sister.

"You'll like him. I know you will."

"Gen, don't take this the wrong way, but just because you're fulfilling some young guy's older woman fantasy doesn't mean I have to like him. Give me some credit, I'll be polite," Hazel said, sounding more callous than she meant. "I mean, I'll make sure to embrace him, figuratively, that is."

"Thanks, I know you will. By the way, Mac's coming tonight."

"Will he be with a young boyfriend too? Oh, geez, I'm sorry again. That wasn't nice," Hazel said, a slight blush of embarrassment spreading across her face. "You know Steve and I always liked Mac. It'll be good to see him. Does he know about Jake?"

"Yes, and he's happy for me. Says I should make up for lost time in the bedroom," Geneva said, testing the sibling waters.

"Really! Please don't feel you have to share that part of your relationship," Hazel said.

"Oh, stop being such a prude. Can't we have a little fun? And Mac is anxious to see you too, but he'll be disappointed that Steve couldn't make it," Geneva said.

"My husband thinks I'm here to see a few Broadway shows with my college roommate. We still keep in touch. How about you? Been to any reunions?"

After an uncomfortable pause, Geneva finally spoke.

"You mean you didn't tell him about my exhibit?"

"No, I didn't feel that was fair," Hazel said, craning her neck to try to find Nikki to bring them another pitcher of milk.

"Not fair? How so? To whom?"

"I didn't want him to feel obligated to come and you

know how much he hates New York," Hazel said, although her excuse sounded flat and watered down.

"But if you had told him, then he could have decided if he wanted to come with you," Geneva said, not willing to drop the subject.

"Isn't it enough that I dragged myself here? Did the two of us have to pay a fortune to fly to New York? The fares are outrageous and who'd look after the kids?" Hazel said, trying to rationalize why she hadn't extended the invitation to her husband, who probably would have been happy to join her.

"Your daughters are teenagers. They drive and they're very responsible. And I told you I'd pay for the tickets."

"Gen, I think I can afford it. This is my husband's busy time of year. He might have felt pressured into coming and I didn't want to stress him out. Besides, you'll have lots of friends at the opening," said Hazel, trying to brighten the moment.

"But you're my family. My only family since Mom passed."

"Steve hates New York. Now can we please talk about something else?"

After a brief pause, Geneva decided not to press further and brought the conversation back to her young boyfriend.

"Oh, I meant to tell you, Jake admired the portrait of us the first time he came up to the loft. He asked me who painted it because he said it didn't look like my style. I told him I had a very talented sister who has a Masters in fine arts, and who spent several years studying in Florence," Geneva said, relieved to close the Steve can of worms.

"Don't feel the need to keep flattering me, but since you've already started, go ahead," Hazel said, with a self-effacing smile.

"It's the truth. You're one of the most gifted artists I've

ever known. You could have branched out a long time ago; even the galleries told you that. I know you don't take my advice, but why wouldn't you listen to the pros?"

"I listened to my conscience. I'm not a commercial artist, and I've never felt the urge to splatter paint around on a mountainous canvas because it's the latest rage. Fine art is just that. If I can't make money from it anymore, that's my problem."

"I assume you're referring to my work. I don't splatter paint around. It takes me weeks to select my colors and a pattern of movement. It's not only opening cans and throwing paint against a canvas," said Geneva. "I wish you'd show a little respect for my method."

"You already know how I feel. Don't make me say anymore," Hazel said.

Nikki had the feeling that all was not going well with the sisters, but when she saw Hazel beckoning her, she stopped by the table with fresh milk and two éclairs. Maybe she'd say something. Her friends always told her that she was a great buffer.

"Here's the milk, if you still need it, and try these. Dad sent them over. So, I guess you're super excited about tonight. I have my outfit all picked out. Geneva, I bet you'll look great, but you know something, and don't take offense, I mean you're pretty and all, but Hazel is gorgeous. I guess you hear that all the time," Nikki said.

"Thank you, Nikki. That's very sweet of you," Hazel said, broadening her perfect smile.

The truth was that even though Geneva was tall and model thin, with a keen sense of style she'd developed from living with Mac, she was no match in beauty for her older sister. Hazel's complexion was the exact peaches-and-cream tone featured in cosmetic ads, seemingly poreless, and her show-stopping, bright blue eyes were envied by anyone who had the pleasure of looking at her. She had a curvy figure, but rarely wore flattering clothing. Even now, she wore a gray business suit with a white shirt, and low heels.

Geneva wore fashion well, due to her height and stick-straight figure, and that was what people noticed when they first met her—not the blemished skin that she camouflaged with heavy makeup, or her thin, fly-away hair tinged with gray that needed constant touching up, as recently noticed by her sister. Hazel's thick, natural auburn locks were shiny and full, something her younger sister had always coveted.

"It's been a pleasure meeting you, Nikki. We'll see you later, but right now, I think my sister and I'd better go back upstairs before I float away. The coffee was excellent, by the way," Hazel said. "What kind is it?"

"Thanks. It's French Roast. Dad gets it decaf from the supplier. Not too many places do that. Glad you enjoyed it. See you guys tonight," Nikki said, and went back to her station.

"Gen, what time do we have to be ready tonight?"

"We should probably leave about seven. The gallery hired a fantastic caterer, you know, for nibbles, so we can eat something there."

"In that case, since we're not having a real dinner, I might as well eat this éclair," Hazel said, and took a healthy bite out of the cream-filled treat.

The sisters walked the half block back home and took the only elevator in the building up to the loft. Once they were inside and seated on the deep, plush sofa, Geneva reiterated how happy she was that Hazel would be with her at the opening.

"I'm thrilled you could make it. I'm very nervous about tonight. It's an important gallery, and some of the top art critics and glitterati will be there. I'll need moral support," she said.

"You? The latest Wonder Woman of the art world? What do you have to be nervous about? You've been featured in other galleries, and your paintings have been selling, so what's the problem?"

"The problem is that these paintings are quite different from the ones that have been successful. If the public shakes its head no tonight, I'm at ground zero. I don't want to go back to my old style."

"I've seen your other work, and frankly, I don't see that much difference," Hazel said, pointing to three canvasses that leaned against the wall. "Those are old style or new?"

"I know you don't appreciate my work, but please, can't you just hold my hand tonight? That's all I'm asking," Geneva said. She took a deep breath and battled on. "Why do we always have to be at each other's throats? Remember how close we used to be as kids? Even in high school, you watched out for me when I was a freshman and you were a junior."

"Sure, I remember those days, let me see, how did it go again? 'The tall pretty one is your sister? How'd you get to be such a shrimp?' Yeah, that was a ton of fun for me," Hazel said.

"Oh please, no one ever called me pretty, and you know you were always the beauty in the family, even in those business suits you insist on wearing. It wasn't all that easy for me in school either, with every teacher you had expecting me to follow in your talented, straight-A footsteps. 'Oh, another Gibson girl and I bet you're every bit as smart as your sister.' I wasn't and they sure found it out in a hurry. While I struggled to pass, you zipped through every subject like lightening," Geneva said, trying to keep the resentment out of her voice.

"Why are we discussing what happened in high school? Let's settle down. I didn't come here to bicker with you, although I'm still pissed that I got stuck with the name Hazel. You were named after a chic city in Switzerland and me, after a witch."

That was one of Hazel's old jokes, but it never failed to get a laugh out of Geneva.

"You can't tell me you hold my name against me! I had no part in that. And anyway, didn't Gwyneth Paltrow or someone famous name one of her kids Hazel? So, see, you're right in style."

"Totally awesome, as Nikki would say. I'll have to call Gwynnie and thank her," Hazel said. "Now, if you don't mind, I'm going to hop in the shower and change for tonight. It's getting late."

While her sister was taking an extremely long shower, Geneva readied a bottle of fine champagne, so they could have a toast before the gallery exhibit. Thoughts of Hazel and Mac drifted through her head as she set up a makeshift bar on the kitchen's high-top table.

She must love the big showerhead that Mac installed. Only the best would do for him. He's been so good to me and I care about his happiness. If I do well tonight I can begin to pay the full maintenance fees here, and I want Hazel to be proud of me. "Oh, there you are. Did you enjoy the shower?" Geneva said, with a wicked knowing smile on her face.

"Who wouldn't? I just sent Steve a text and pictures with the name of the showerhead so he can get it for our bathroom, although Lord knows I'll have to hire a plumber to do the work, but it'll be worth it. It's like being in a rainforest. And those products! Hope you don't mind that I used everything I could get my hands on, and thanks for leaving me a robe. I forgot to pack mine," Hazel said, her wet hair layering down around her shoulders.

"No problem. Mac has the bath boutique deliver that stuff to me because he knows otherwise I'd be using laundry soap," Geneva said. "We still have time before we leave and I cracked open a bottle of champagne. Let's celebrate before the exhibit because there might not be anything to celebrate for afterwards. So, what are you going to wear?"

While Geneva poured champagne into the vintage coupe glasses Mac had insisted she keep, her sister brought out the outfit she had planned for the evening.

"How's this?" Hazel said, holding up a navy suit with another white blouse.

"It looks like what you were wearing. You're not going on a job interview. Couldn't you have brought along a cocktail dress?" Geneva said, her excitement waning because of her sister's apparent disinterest in the evening ahead.

"I don't wear those much to go out for pizza and a movie. Besides, you're the glamour girl. I saw that gold silk number in the closet. You're going to look like the Oscar. Oh, stop pouting, I'm only kidding. You'll look like you always do, only with a little more glitz than usual."

"Sometimes I swear you downplay your looks just to make me feel guilty. Even Nikki thought you were 'awesome' so don't make yourself out to be the downtrodden older sister. Come on, have a glass of champagne with me," Geneva said.

"No thanks. I had enough sugar with that éclair, which I have to admit was superb and totally worth the calories," Hazel said.

"I refuse to toast by myself. Just take a few sips. It won't kill you."

Hazel grabbed the glass and downed half the bubbly wine. "There, now are you happy? I can feel a migraine starting already."

Geneva silently counted to ten before speaking.

"Tonight is so important to me and I'm very grateful you're here. Couldn't you at least pretend to be happy for me?"

"What do you want from me? I'm here, aren't I? Of course, I'm happy for you. I'm your sister."

"Wait a minute. That's right. You are my sister. Sometimes I forget, you'll have to forgive me," Geneva muttered, half under her breath, but loud and sarcastic enough for Hazel to hear.

"What was that?"

"You're my sister. I love you. That's all," Geneva said sharply, and not at all lovingly.

"Well, if you love me so much then pour me another glass. I don't get headaches from the good stuff and this must have cost a fortune. Then I'm going to dry my hair, put on some makeup and my 'business' suit. For some unearthly reason, we wear the same size shoe, so if you have a fancy pair you can lend me, I'll pretend to be Cinderella for the evening," Hazel said, sipping the champagne. "Come on, we need to get going. I don't think it's chic to be late for your own opening."

"We never say that to each other, you know. I love you."

"Gen, please, what is it now? Don't push me," Hazel said.

"How is that pushing you? To say you love your sister? You say it all the time to Steve, and the kids. I've heard you. You've never once said it to me," Geneva said, pouring herself another blast of the champagne that Mac had sent over with a note of congratulations. At least he had confidence in her. Jake thought everything she did was brilliant, but he was her boyfriend, not an art critic. If only her sister believed in her.

"Come on, let's get moving," Hazel said, and tipped the last of the golden liquid into the old-fashioned glass.

It was hours later that the two women once again rode the elevator up to the fourth floor loft, only this time instead of exchanging glowering looks and being at cross purposes, they were giggling like two school girls. Geneva was holding on to her sparkly sandals while Hazel was still teetering on the borrowed silver stilettos.

"Thank the good Lord we didn't have to drive home," Hazel said, once they entered the loft and flopped down on the sofa.

"One of the advantages of living in Manhattan. Taxis. And when did your hair get all spiky and gelled, and with pink streaks?"

"Nikki brought the stuff with her. She said it would make me look hot," Hazel said, collapsing into a peal of laughter.

Hazel kicked off the designer shoes and sprawled out against the down-filled throw pillows on the sofa. "Well, you did it," she said, after making herself comfortable.

"I really did, didn't I?"

"I should say so. To my count, the gallery sold eight pieces by the time the caviar disappeared. I guess Ritz crackers and Velveeta wouldn't cut it with this crowd."

"Speaking of disappearing acts, what happened to the white shirt you had on under your suit?" Geneva said.

"Jake suggested the suit would look dressier without the blouse, so I took it off in the ladies room," Hazel said.

"I see. Jake, huh."

"Yes, your young man. He's as sweet as you said, and a whole lot more, including being a major flirt. Oh, don't worry, he's crazy about you, but he did say that if he'd met me first you'd have had some competition."

"And that was before or after he asked you to remove your blouse? But honestly, he's terrific, isn't he? I know he's young…" Geneva said.

"Gen, you don't become soul mates overnight. Steve and I dated for two years before we got married and our first date was an abomination. All he did was talk about himself for hours, but I have to admit the chemistry was there, and it worked out for us. Maybe you should give more thought to a relationship with Jake. I mean fifteen years isn't impossible to deal with and if it were the other way around, there wouldn't even be a discussion," Hazel said, getting up to see if she could find another bottle of champagne in the fridge.

"I can't believe you're saying this. He must have made quite an impression on you," Geneva said, following her sister into the kitchen.

"Oh, he did alright, and he asked if I were your younger sister!"

"We're not even three years apart. Anyone could make that mistake," Geneva said, pretending to be a little jealous. She knew Hazel would never make a play for any man other than her husband. She could deal with some harmless flirting.

"I guess because I've been married and a mother for so many years I seem much older than you."

"Well, you sexy thing, right now you look like you're about sixteen. I was so happy and proud you were with me tonight."

"I'm proud of you, too. Any more of that bubbly? Oh, here it is. You mind?"

"Be my guest and pour two while you're at it. We deserve it," Geneva said. "Let's sit back down because there's an idea I've been thinking about that I want to run by you."

"At this hour? I've got a plane to catch in the morning," Hazel said, not sure she was sober enough to understand any kind of an idea, as she followed Geneva back to the sofa where they parked themselves for the discussion.

"What would you say if you and I opened our own

gallery in New York, provided I could find affordable space?" Geneva said.

"I'd say you were nuts, but go ahead. Let me hear the rest of this plan while I still have the booze in me."

"We could both show our work, or maybe take in some pieces on consignment to help pay expenses. I know you and Steve wouldn't move to New York, but I'd run it and you could come up whenever you felt like it. Our different styles would make it that much more interesting, and we could call the gallery Two Sisters. Like the portrait. You're not saying anything. Does that mean you'll think about it? Maybe even a pinch?"

"Two Sisters, huh? Wow, that'll bring 'em in," Hazel said.

"We'll think of something better."

"And maybe portraits will make a comeback, that is, when pigs fly."

"I'm betting that when people see our portrait in the window they'll all want one," Geneva said.

"Yeah, maybe of their dogs. I hear that's big."

"Why don't you sleep on it. I wish you could stay a few more days."

Hazel put her glass down and turned to face her sister.

"I can't this time, but I promise I'll be back soon. With Steve, that is, if you don't mind giving up your room again."

"With Steve? Of course I wouldn't mind, but why would he want to come if he hates New York?"

"He may hate New York but he loves real estate, and frankly, Gen, you shouldn't have to make a deal for gallery space by yourself. There's way too much involved, and it's Steve's specialty."

"I guess I'd have to ask Mac, but he already does so much for me. I think you're right; it'd be great if Steve could help us after I do some legwork. Does that mean you're going to consider it?" Geneva said, growing sleepy from the champagne and the excitement of the evening.

"Oh, why not? It's time I picked up a paintbrush again and if portraits aren't selling, then I'll do nature scenes. People still like cows and the beach, don't they?" Hazel said, getting up from the sofa.

"In the same painting? That'd probably be the next big thing," she said, joking around. "I'd better get to bed. I have to leave pretty early in the morning. Thanks for giving up your bedroom. And don't forget to give me the website of that bath boutique. I'm definitely buying the same shampoo when I get home and all the other stuff. Whew, I am wiped!"

"I'm exhausted, too. Get a good night's rest and we'll talk in the morning."

"Gen, call me anytime. I want to hear everything—about the gallery space and the boyfriend, so even if I'm at the mall, I'll pick up, but my next shopping trip is to the art supply store if we're going into business."

Geneva stood up next to her sister, who no longer had the extra height with her heels off, and put her arms around her. It was an awkward stance, since Geneva towered over her, but Hazel found a way to wrap her arms around her sister.

"I will, and you have to promise that you'll let me know what's going on in your life. Let's be friends," Geneva said, releasing her grip.

"Friends? We're sisters, or have you forgotten that again?" Hazel said, as she walked to the bedroom. At the door, she turned and held up her hand. "Hold on there. I have something else to tell you."

"Yes?" said Geneva, expecting she would finally hear the three words she'd asked about earlier in the day.

"Try adding a little yellow to your greens. It'll add more contrast to your backgrounds."

"Thanks. Sleep well," Geneva said, trying to keep the disappointment out of her voice.

"Oh, what's wrong with me? All that champagne has muddled my mind. There is something else I've been meaning to tell you," Hazel said, a sly look on her face. "I love you, Sis. I'm glad I came. Go to sleep."

ACKNOWLEDGMENTS

To the many readers who enjoyed the stories in my first published collection, *Sitting Pretty,* and encouraged me to write a second one. To the National League of American Pen Women, Florida Mystery Writers, Women's National Book Association, South Florida Theater League and Murder on the Beach Mystery Bookstore for keeping me focused and sparked with energy to continue with my craft. To director Steven Strickland, who brought many of these stories to life on the Off-Broadway stage. To my Lifeboat Group who made sure I took enough breaks from work to enjoy the world around me. To Huck, Loie, Ruby, Sadie and the rest of my family for keeping me perpetually amused. To Penelope Love, my editor, for her support and commitment to me as a client and friend.

Thank you for reading **Coffee Breaks**. *If you enjoyed this book, please support the author's efforts by helping other readers find this book. Here are some suggestions for your consideration:*

* Write an online customer review.

* Gift a copy of this book to a booklover friend.

* Visit Carol's website or email her at
polowhite@aol.com

www.carolwhitefiction.com

* Spread the word about her work. Suggest her titles to a local book club.

* For group orders of ten books or more, contact Citrine Publishing at (561) 299-1150 or Publisher@CitrinePublishing.com.

www.ingramcontent.com/pod-product-compliance
Lightning Source LLC
Chambersburg PA
CBHW050526260626
47157CB00004B/1488